*Annie wanted...*

## TRADING *places*

*...Lydia wanted the spotlight.*

*They both found love....*

**This month:** *Her Desert Dream*

Girl-next-door Lydia Young trades places with Lady
Napier for a week! Look-alike Lydia thinks
that a holiday in the desert kingdom of
Ramal Hamrah with a gorgeous sheikh
doesn't sound like much of a chore!

**Last month:** *Christmas Angel for the Billionaire*

Lady Annie Napier has been in the media spotlight
most of her life, especially since taking over her
parents' charity work. Now Annie
wants a break from being the "nation's angel,"
so she goes undercover....

Available at eHarlequin.com

Step into a world of stars and sand,
deserts and dreams…

**Welcome to Bab el Sama:**
a place steeped in magic where you can
unlock the mysteries of the desert…

**Visit the souk:**
heady with the scent of jasmine,
it's an absolute treasure of gold, silks, spices.

**Enter the sheikh's world:**
princesses draped in the finest silks, palaces adorned
with the purest gold, luxury at every fingertip.

**Meet Sheikh Kalil al-Zaki:**
a man of the land, a king of his people.

**Turn the pages**
and step into a desert dream….

# LIZ FIELDING

*Her Desert Dream*

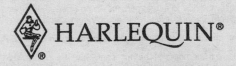

TORONTO • NEW YORK • LONDON
AMSTERDAM • PARIS • SYDNEY • HAMBURG
STOCKHOLM • ATHENS • TOKYO • MILAN • MADRID
PRAGUE • WARSAW • BUDAPEST • AUCKLAND

Recycling programs
for this product may
not exist in your area.

ISBN-13: 978-0-373-17626-7

HER DESERT DREAM

First North American Publication 2009.

**Liz Fielding** was born with itchy feet. She made it to Zambia before her twenty-first birthday and, gathering her own special hero and a couple of children on the way, lived in Botswana, Kenya and Bahrain—with pauses for sightseeing pretty much everywhere in between. She finally came to a full stop in a tiny Welsh village cradled by misty hills, and these days she mostly leaves her pen to do the traveling. When she's not sorting out the lives and loves of her characters, she potters in the garden, reads her favorite authors and spends a lot of time wondering "What if…?" For news of upcoming books—and to sign up for her occasional newsletter—visit Liz's Web site at www.lizfielding.com.

# CHAPTER ONE

LYDIA YOUNG was a fake from the tip of her shoes to the saucy froth of feathers on her hat but, as she held centre stage at a reception in a swanky London hotel, she had the satisfaction of knowing that she was the best there was.

Her suit, an interpretation of a designer original, had been run up at home by her mother, but her mother had once been a seamstress at a couturier house. And while her shoes, bag and wristwatch were knock-offs, they were the finest knock-offs that money could buy. The kind that only someone intimate with the real thing would clock without a very close look. But they were no more than the window dressing.

She'd once heard an actress describe how she built a character from the feet up and she had taken that lesson to heart.

Lydia had studied her character's walk, her gestures, a certain tilt of the head. She'd worked on the voice until it was her own and the world famous smile—a slightly toned down version of the mile-wide one that came as naturally as breathing—was, even if she said it herself, a work of art.

Her reward was that when she walked into a room full of people who knew that she was a lookalike, hired by the hour to lend glamour to the opening of a club or a restaurant or to appear at the launch of a new product, there was absolutely nothing in her appearance or manner to jar the fantasy and, as a result, she was treated with the same deference as the real thing.

She was smiling now as she mixed and mingled, posing for photographs with guests at a product launch being held at the kind of hotel that in her real life she would only glimpse from a passing bus.

Would the photographs be framed? she wondered. Placed on mantels, so that their neighbours, friends would believe that they'd actually met 'England's Sweetheart'?

Someone spoke to her and she offered her hand, the smile, asked all the right questions, chatting as naturally as if to the stately home born.

A dozen more handshakes, a few more photographs as the managing director of the company handed her a blush-pink rose that was as much a part of her character's image as the smile and then it was over. Time to go back to her real world. A hospital appointment for her mother, then an evening shift at the 24/7 supermarket where she might even be shelving the new brand of tea that was being launched today.

There was a certain irony in that, she thought as she approached the vast marble entrance lobby, heading for the cloakroom to transform herself back into plain Lydia Young for the bus ride home. Anticipating the head-turning ripple of awareness as she passed.

People had been turning to look, calling out 'Rose' to her in the street since she was a teen. The likeness had been striking, much more than the colour of her hair, the even features, vivid blue eyes that were eerily like those of the sixteen-year-old Lady Rose. And she had played up to it, copying her hairstyle, begging her mother to make her a copy of the little black velvet jacket Lady Rose had been wearing in the picture that had appeared on the front page of every newspaper the day after her sixteenth birthday. Copying her 'look', just as her mother's generation had slavishly followed another young princess.

Who wouldn't want to look like an icon?

A photograph taken by the local paper had brought her to the attention of the nation's biggest 'lookalike' agency and overnight being 'Lady Rose' had not only given her wheel-chair-bound mother a new focus in life as she'd studied the clothes, hunted down fabrics to reproduce them, but had provided extra money to pay the bills, pay for her driving lessons. She'd even saved up enough to start looking for a car so that she could take her mum further than the local shops.

Lost in the joy of that thought, Lydia was halfway across the marble entrance before she realised that no one was looking at her. That someone else was the centre of attention.

Her stride faltered as that 'someone' turned and she came face to face with herself. Or, more accurately, the self she was pretending to be.

Lady Roseanne Napier.

England's Sweetheart.

In person.

From the tip of her mouth-wateringly elegant hat, to the toes of her matching to-die-for shoes.

And Lydia, whose heart had joined her legs in refusing to move, could do nothing but pray for the floor to open up and swallow her.

The angel in charge of rescuing fools from moments of supreme embarrassment clearly had something more pressing to attend to. The marble remained solid and it was Lady Rose, the corner of her mouth lifting in a wry little smile, who saved the day.

'I know the face,' she said, extending her hand, 'but I'm afraid the name escapes me.'

'Lydia, madam, Lydia Young' she stuttered as she grasped it, more for support than to shake hands.

Should she curtsy? Women frequently forgot themselves sufficiently to curtsy to her but she wasn't sure her knees, once down, would ever make it back up again and the situation was quite bad enough without turning it into a farce.

Then, realising that she was still clutching the slender hand much too tightly, she let go, stammered out an apology.

'I'm s-so sorry. I promise this wasn't planned. I had no idea you'd be here.'

'Please, it's not a problem,' Lady Rose replied sympathetically, kindness itself as she paused long enough to exchange a few words, ask her what she was doing at the hotel, put her at her ease. Then, on the point of rejoining the man waiting for her at the door—the one the newspapers were saying Lady Rose would marry—she looked back. 'As a matter of interest, Lydia, how much do you charge for being me? Just in case I ever decided to take a day off?'

'No charge for you, Lady Rose. Just give me a call. Any time.'

'I don't suppose you fancy three hours of Wagner this evening?' she asked, but before Lydia could reply, she shook her head. 'Just kidding. I wouldn't wish that on you.'

The smile was in place, the voice light with laughter, but for a moment her eyes betrayed her and Lydia saw beyond the fabulous clothes, the pearl choker at her throat. Lady Rose, she realised, was a woman in trouble and, taking a card from the small clutch bag she was holding, she offered it to her.

'I meant what I said. Call me,' Lydia urged. 'Any time.'

Three weeks later, when she answered her cellphone, a voice she knew as well as her own said, 'Did you mean it?'

Kalil al-Zaki stared down into the bare winter garden of his country's London Embassy, watching the Ambassador's children racing around in the care of their nanny.

He was only a couple of years younger than his cousin. By the time a man was in his thirties he should have a family, sons…

'I know how busy you are, but it's just for a week, Kal.'

'I don't understand the problem,' he said, clamping down on the bitterness, the anger that with every passing day came closer to spilling over, and turned from the children to their mother, his cousin's lovely wife, Princess Lucy al-Khatib. 'Nothing is going to happen to Lady Rose at Bab el Sama.'

As it was the personal holiday complex of the Ramal

Hamrahn royal family, security would, he was certain, be state-of-the-art.

'Of course it isn't,' Lucy agreed, 'but her grandfather came to see me yesterday. Apparently there has been a threat against her.'

He frowned. 'A threat? What kind of threat?'

'He refused to go into specifics.'

'Well, that was helpful.' Then, 'So why did he come to you rather than Hanif?'

'I was the one who offered her the use of our Bab el Sama cottage whenever she needed to get away from it all.' She barely lifted her shoulders, but it was unmistakably a shrug. 'The Duke's line is that he doesn't want to alarm her.'

*Line?*

'He thought the simplest solution would be if I made some excuse and withdrew the invitation.'

The one thing that Kal could do was read women—with a mother, two stepmothers and more sisters than he could count, he'd had a lot of practise—and he recognised an *as if* shrug when he saw one.

'You believe he's making a fuss about nothing.'

'He lost his son and daughter-in-law in the most brutal manner and it's understandable that he's protective of his granddaughter. She wasn't even allowed to go to school…'

'Lucy!' he snapped. This all round the houses approach was unlike her. And why on earth she should think he'd want to babysit some spoiled celebrity 'princess', he couldn't imagine. But Lucy was not the enemy. On the contrary. 'I'm sorry.'

'I've no doubt there's been something,' she said, dismissing his apology with an elegant gesture. 'Everyone in the public eye gets their share of crank mail, but…' there it was, the *but* word '…I doubt it's more than some delusional creature getting hot under the collar over rumours that she's about to announce her engagement to Rupert Devenish.'

'You're suggesting that it's no more than a convenient excuse to apply pressure on you, keep her under the paternal eye?' He didn't believe it. The woman wasn't a child; she had to be in her mid-twenties.

'Maybe I'm being unjust.' She sighed. 'I might believe that the man is obsessively controlling, but I have no doubt that Rose is very precious to him.'

'And not just him.' He might suspect the public image of purity and goodness was no more than a well-managed PR exercise, but it was one the media were happy to buy into, at least until they had something more salacious to print on their front pages. 'You do realise that if anything were to happen to Lady Roseanne Napier while she's in Ramal Hamrah, the British press would be merciless?' And he would be the one held to blame.

'Meanwhile, they'll happily invade her privacy on a daily basis in the hope of getting intimate pictures of her for no better reason than to boost the circulation of their grubby little rags.'

'They can only take pictures of what she does,' he pointed out.

'So she does nothing.'

'Nothing?' He frowned. 'Really? She really is as pure, as angelic as the media would have us believe?'

'It's not something to be sneered at, Kalil.' Her turn to snap. 'She's been in the public eye since she was dubbed the "people's angel" on her sixteenth birthday. She hasn't been able to move a finger for the last ten years without someone taking a photograph of her.'

'Then she has my sympathy.'

'She doesn't need your sympathy, Kal. What she's desperate for is some privacy. Time on her own to sort out where she's going from here.'

'I thought you said she was getting married.'

'I said there were rumours to that effect, fuelled, I have no doubt, by the Duke,' she added, this time making no attempt to hide her disapproval. 'There comes a point at which a virginal image stops being charming, special and instead becomes the butt of cruel humour. Marriage, babies will keep the story moving forward and His Grace has lined up an Earl in waiting to fill this bill.'

'An arranged marriage?' It was his turn to shrug. 'Is that so bad?' In his experience, it beat the ramshackle alternative of love hands down. 'What does Hanif say?'

'In his opinion, if there had been a genuine threat the Duke would have made a formal approach through the Foreign Office instead of attempting to bully me into withdrawing my invitation.'

With considerably more success, Kal thought.

'Even so,' he replied, 'it might be wiser to do everyone a favour and tell Lady Rose that the roof has fallen in at your holiday cottage.'

'In other words, knuckle under, make life easy for ourselves? What about Rose? They give her no peace, Kal.'

'She's never appeared to want it,' he pointed out. Barely a week went by without her appearance on the front pages of the newspapers or some gossip magazine.

'Would it make any difference if she did?' She shook her head, not expecting an answer. 'Will you go with her, Kal? While I don't believe Rose is in any actual danger, I daren't risk leaving her without someone to watch her back and if I have to ask your uncle to detail an Emiri guard, she'll simply be exchanging one prison for another.'

'Prison?'

'What would you call it?' She reached out, took his hand. 'I'm desperately worried about her. On the surface she's so serene, but underneath there's a desperation...' She shook her head. 'Distract her, Kal. Amuse her, make her laugh.'

'Do you want me to protect her or make love to her?' he asked, with just the slightest edge to his voice. He'd done his best to live down the playboy image that clung to the al-Zaki name, but he would always be the grandson of an exiled playboy prince, the son of a man whose pursuit of beautiful women had kept the gossip writers happily in business for forty years.

Building an international company from the floor up, supporting Princess Lucy's charities, didn't make the kind of stories that sold newspapers.

'Consider this as a diplomatic mission, Kal,' Lucy replied enigmatically, 'and a diplomat is a man who manages to give everyone what they want while serving the needs of his own country. You do want to serve your country?' she asked.

They both knew that he had no country, but clearly Lucy saw this as a way to promote his cause. The restoration of his family to their rightful place. His marriage to the precious daughter of one of the great Ramal Hamrahn families. And, most important of all, to take his dying grandfather home. For that, he would play nursemaid to an entire truckload of aristocratic virgins.

'Princess,' he responded with the slightest bow, 'rest assured that I will do everything in my power to ensure that Lady Roseanne Napier enjoys her visit to Ramal Hamrah.'

'Thank you, Kal. I can now assure the Duke that, since the Emir's nephew is to take personal care of her security, he can have no worries about her safety.'

Kal shook his head, smiling despite himself. 'You won't, I imagine, be telling him which nephew?'

'Of course I'll tell him,' she replied. 'How else will he be able to thank your uncle for the service you have rendered him?'

'You think he'll be grateful?'

'Honestly? I think he'll be chewing rocks, but he's not about to insult the Emir of Ramal Hamrah by casting doubt on the character of one of his family. Even one whose grandfather tried to start a revolution.'

'And how do you suppose His Highness will react?'

'He will have no choice but to ask his wife to pay a courtesy visit on their distinguished visitor,' she replied. 'The opportunity to meet your aunt is the best I can do for you, Kal. The rest is up to you.'

'Lucy...' He was for a moment lost for words. 'How can I...'

She simply raised a finger to her lips, then said, 'Just take care of Rose for me.'

'How on earth did you swing a week off just before Christmas, Lydie?'

'Pure charm,' she replied, easing her shoulder as she handed over her checkout at the end of her shift. That and a cross-her-heart promise to the manager that she'd use the time to think seriously about the management course he'd been nagging her to take for what seemed like forever. He'd been totally supportive of her lookalike career, allowing her to be flexible in her shifts, but he wanted her to start thinking about the future, a real career.

'Well, remember us poor souls chained to the checkout listening to *Jingle Bells* for the umpteenth time, while you're lying in the sun, won't you?'

'You've got to be kidding,' she replied, with the grin of a woman with a week in the sun ahead of her.

And it was true; this was going to be an unbelievable experience. Rose had offered her the chance of a dream holiday in the desert. An entire week of undiluted luxury in which she was going to be wearing designer clothes—not copies run up by her mother—and treated like a real princess. Not some fake dressed up to look like one.

The euphoria lasted until she reached her car.

She'd told her colleagues at work that she'd been invited to spend a week at a friend's holiday apartment, which was near enough to the truth, but she hadn't told a soul where she was really going, not even her mother, and that had been hard.

Widowed in the same accident that had left her confined to

a wheelchair, Lydia's 'Lady Rose' gigs were the highlight of her mother's life and normally they shared all the planning, all the fun, and her mother's friends all joined vicariously in the excitement.

But this was different. This wasn't a public gig. The slightest hint of what she was doing would ruin everything for Rose. She knew that her mother wouldn't be able to resist sharing such an incredible secret with her best friend who'd be staying with her while she was away. She might as well have posted a bulletin on the wall of her Facebook page.

Instead, she'd casually mentioned a woman at work who was looking for a fourth person to share a last-minute apartment deal in Cyprus—which was true—and left it to her mother to urge her to grab it.

Which of course she had.

'Why don't you go, love?' she'd said, right on cue. 'All the hours you work, you deserve a break. Jennie will stop with me while you're away.'

That the two of them would have a great time together, gossiping non-stop, did nothing to make Lydia feel better about the deception.


Kal had been given less than twenty-four hours to make arrangements for his absence, pack and visit the clinic where his grandfather was clinging to life to renew the promise he'd made that he should die in the place he still called home.

Now, as he stood at the steps of the jet bearing the Emir's personal insignia, he wondered what His Highness's reaction had been when he'd learned who would be aboard it today.

It wasn't his first trip to the country that his great-grandfather had once ruled. Like his grandfather and his father, Kalil was forbidden from using his title, using the name Khatib, but, unlike the old man, he was not an exile.

He'd bought a waterfront apartment in the capital, Rumaillah. His aircraft flew a regular freight service into Ramal Hamrah, despite the fact that they remained stubbornly empty. No one would dare offend the Emir by using Kalzak Air Services and he made no effort to break the embargo. He did not advertise his services locally, or compete for business. He kept his rates equal to, but not better than his competitors. Took the loss.

This was not about profit but establishing his right to be there.

He'd been prepared to be patient, sit it out, however long it took, while he'd quietly worked on the restoration of his family home at Umm al Sama. But he'd continued to remain invisible to the ruling family, his family, a stranger in his own country, and patience was no longer an option. Time was running out for his grandfather and nothing mattered but bringing him home to die.

He'd do anything. Even babysit a wimp of a woman who wasn't, apparently, allowed to cross the road without someone holding her hand.

He identified himself to Security, then to the cabin crew, who were putting the final touches to the kind of luxury few airline passengers would ever encounter.

His welcome was reserved, but no one reeled back in horror.

A steward took his bag, introduced him to Atiya Bishara, who would be taking care of Lady Rose during the flight, then gave him a full tour of the aircraft so that he could check for himself that everything was in order.

He was treated no differently from any anonymous security officer who'd been asked to escort Lady Rose on a flight that, historically, should have been his grandfather's to command. Which said pretty much everything he needed to know about how the rest of the week was likely to pan out.

His aunt might pay a courtesy visit to Lady Rose, but even if she acknowledged his presence it would be as a servant.

Lydia rapidly exchanged clothes with Rose in the private room that had been set aside for her as guest of honour at the Pink Ribbon Lunch.

Lady Rose had walked into the room; ten minutes later Lydia, heart pounding, mouth dry, had walked out in her place.

She held her breath as a dark-suited security man fell in behind her.

Would he really be fooled? Rose had assured her that he would be looking everywhere but at her, but even wearing Rose's crushed raspberry silk suit, a saucy matching hat with a wispy veil and the late Duchess of Oldfield's famous pearl choker, it seemed impossible that he wouldn't notice the difference.

But there was no challenge.

Smile, she reminded herself as she approached the hotel manager who was waiting to escort her to the door. It was just another job. And, holding that thought, she offered the man her hand, thanked him for doing such a good job for the Pink Ribbon Club, before stepping outside into the thin winter sunshine.

Rose had warned her what to expect but, since rumours of a wedding had started to circulate, media interest had spiralled out of control. Nothing could have prepared her for the noise, the flashes from dozens of cameras. And it wasn't just the paparazzi lined up on the footpath. There were dozens of ordinary people hoping for a glance of the 'people's angel', all of them taking pictures, video, with their cellphones. People who thought she was the real thing, deserved the real thing, and she had to remind herself not just to smile, but to breathe.

It was the photographers who saved her, calling out, 'Lady Rose! This way, Lady Rose! Love the hat, Lady Rose!'

The eye-catching little hat had been made specially for the occasion. Fashioned from a stiffened loop of the same material as the suit, it had a dark pink net veil scattered with tiny velvet ribbon loops that skimmed her face, breaking up the outline, blurring any slight differences that might be picked out by an eagle-eyed picture editor.

Breathe, smile…

'How was lunch, Lady Rose?' one of the photographers called out.

She swallowed down the nervous lump in her throat and said, 'It was a wonderful lunch for a great cause.' Then, when there was still no challenge, no one pointed a finger, shouted, *Fake!*, she added, 'The Pink Ribbon Club.' And, growing in confidence, she lifted her right hand so that the diamond and amethyst ring on her right hand flashed in the sunlight as she pointedly touched the little ribbon-shaped hat. 'Don't forget to mention it.'

'Are you looking forward to your holiday, Lady Rose?'

Growing in confidence—it was true, apparently, that people saw only what they expected to see—she picked out the photographer who'd asked the question and smiled directly at him.

'Very much,' she said.

'Will you be on your own?' he dared.

'Only if you all take the week off, too,' she replied, raising a laugh. Yes! She could do this! And, turning her back on the photographers, she walked down the steps and crossed to the real people, just as she had seen Lady Rose do a hundred times on news clips. Had done herself at promotional gigs.

She took the flowers they handed her, stopped to answer questions—she could have entered *Mastermind* with Lady Rose as her specialist subject—paused for photographs, overwhelmed by the genuine warmth with which people reached out to her. To Rose…

'Madam…' The security officer touched his watch, indicating that it was time to leave.

She gave the crowd a final wave and smile and turned back to the limousine, stepped inside. The door closed behind her and, within moments, she was gliding through London behind a liveried chauffeur.

At which point she bit back a giggle.

This wasn't like any other job. No way. At this point, if it had been an ordinary job, she'd be heading for the hotel cloakroom for a quick change before catching the bendy bus back to work. Instead, she was in a top-of-the-range Mercedes, heading for an airfield used by people for whom the private jet was the only way to travel. The final hurdle before she could relax and enjoy being Lady Rose without the risk of someone taking a second look and challenging her.

It was a thought to bring the giggle under control. Not the fear of being challenged. The thought of getting in a plane.

Kal paced the VIP lounge, certain that he was wasting his time.

Lucy was wrong. Playing nanny to a woman known to the world as 'England's Sweetheart', or 'angel' or even *'virgin'*, for heaven's sake, wasn't going to make him any friends in the Ramal Hamrahn court. Unless there really was an attempt on her life and he saved her. Maybe he should arrange one...

He stopped fantasising and checked the time.

Another minute and she'd be late. No more than he'd expected. She was probably still posing for photographs, being feted by her fans.

He'd seen her on the news—she was impossible to avoid—a pale, spun-sugar confection, all sweetness and light. He knew she was a friend of Lucy's but, really, could anyone be that perfect?

He was about to pick up a newspaper, settle down to wait, when a stir at the entrance alerted him to her arrival. That she had arrived exactly on schedule should have been a point in her favour. It only served to irritate him further.

Lydia could not believe the ease with which she moved through airport formalities but when you were an A-list VIP, related to the Queen, even if it was goodness knew how many times removed, it seemed that the ordinary rules did not apply. Forget the usual hassle with the luggage trolley. She hadn't even seen the bags that Rose had packed for this trip.

And no one was going to make her line up at a check-in desk. Clearly, people who flew in their own private jets did not expect to queue for *anything*.

She didn't have to take off her jacket and shoes, surrender

the handbag and briefcase she was carrying to be X-rayed. Instead, she was nodded through the formalities and escorted to the departure lounge by Lady Rose's security officer.

Rose had explained that he would see her to the aircraft and after that she'd be on her own, free from all risk of discovery. And once she was in Ramal Hamrah, ensconced in the luxury of Princess Lucy's holiday cottage at Bab el Sama, all she had to do was put in the occasional appearance in the garden or on the beach to ensure that the paparazzi were able to snatch pictures of her while she lived like a princess for a week.

It was like some dream-come-true fairy tale. Checkout girl to princess. Pure Cinderella.

All she needed was a pair of glass slippers and a fairy god-mother to provide her with someone tall, dark and handsome to play Prince Charming.

She wouldn't even have to flee when the clock struck twelve. She had a whole week before she turned back into Lydia Young, whose job as supermarket checkout girl was occasionally enlivened by a lookalike gig.

She automatically reached for the door to the VIP departure lounge, but it opened as she approached; a 'Lady' with a capital L did not open doors for herself. She was so intent on covering her mistake by adjusting the veil on her hat that she missed the fact that her escort had stopped at the door.

'Mr al-Zaki will take care of you from here, madam.'

Who?

She thought the word, but never voiced it.

All sound seemed to fade away as she looked up. She was tall, but the knee-meltingly gorgeous man waiting to 'take care' of her was half a head taller and as his eyes, dark and intense, locked with hers, she felt the jolt of it to her knees. And yes, no doubt about it, her knees melted as he lowered his head briefly, said, 'Kalil al-Zaki, Lady Rose,' introducing himself with the utmost formality. 'Princess Lucy has asked me to ensure that your holiday is all that you wish.'

Graceful, beautiful, contained power rippling beneath exquisite tailoring, he was, she thought crazily, the embodiment of Bagheera, the bold, reckless panther from her childhood favourite, *The Jungle Book*. She'd made her father read over and over the description of his coat like watered silk, his voice as soft as wild honey dripping from a tree.

Her own, as she struggled for a suitable response, was nonexistent.

Kalil al-Zaki might favour well-cut British tailoring over a fancy Ruritanian uniform but he was as close to her own Prince Charming fantasy as she was ever likely to come and she had to resist the temptation to look around for the old lady with wings and a wand who'd been listening in on her thoughts.

# CHAPTER TWO

'YOU'RE coming with me to Bab el Sama?' she managed finally, knowing that she should be horrified by this turn of events. The frisson of excitement rippling through her suggested that she was anything but.

'There and back,' he confirmed. 'My instructions are to keep you safe from harm. I have a letter of introduction from Princess Lucy, but the aircraft is waiting and the pilot will not wish to miss his slot. If you're ready to board?'

Lydia just about managed a nod and the noise flooded back like a shock wave as, his hand curling possessively around her elbow, he walked her to the door, across the tarmac towards the plane. Where she received shock number two.

When Rose had explained that she'd be flying in a private jet, Lydia had anticipated one of those small executive jobs. The reality was a full-sized passenger aircraft bearing the royal livery.

She'd fantasized about being treated like a princess, but this was the real deal; all that was missing was the red carpet and a guard of honour.

If they found out she was a fake they were not going to be amused and, as Kalil al-Zaki's touch sizzled through her sleeve, Lydia had to concentrate very hard on marshalling her knees and putting one foot in front of the other.

This was anything but a fairy tale and if she fell flat on her face there would be no fairy godmother to rescue her with the wave of a wand.

Concentrate, concentrate…

She'd already had an encounter with one of Rose's security guards. He hadn't looked at her the way that Kalil al-Zaki had looked and he certainly hadn't touched. The closest he'd been was when he'd opened the car door and his eyes had not been on her, but the crowd.

No matter what he said about 'keeping her safe', it was clear that this man was not your standard bodyguard, so who on earth was he?

Should she have recognised his name?

Think…

He'd mentioned Princess Lucy. So far, so clear. She was the friend who'd lent Rose her holiday 'cottage' for the week. The wife of the Emir's youngest son, who was the Ramal Hamrahn Ambassador to London.

Rose had filled her in on all the important background details, a little of their history, the names and ages of their children, so that she wouldn't make a mistake if any of the staff at Bab el Sama mentioned her or her children.

But that was it.

This was supposed to be no more than a walk-on role with only servants and the occasional telephoto lens for company.

A few minutes performing for a bunch of journalists, and getting away with it, had given her a terrific buzz, but playing the part convincingly under the eyes of someone like Kalil al-Zaki for an entire week was a whole different ball game.

Hopefully, the letter of introduction would fill in the details, she thought as his hand fell away at the top of the steps and she was greeted by the waiting stewardess.

'Welcome aboard the royal flight, Lady Rose. I am Atiya Bishara and I will be taking care of you today.' Then, looking at the flowers she was clutching like a lifeline, 'Shall I put those in water?'

Lydia, back on more or less familiar territory, began to breathe again. This was the basic lookalike stuff she'd been doing since she was fifteen years old and she managed to go through the standard 'How d'you do?' routine as she surrendered the flowers and the dark pink leather briefcase that exactly matched her hat. The one Rose had used to conceal the cash she'd needed for her week away and which now contained Lydia's own essentials, including her own passport in the event that anything went wrong.

'Your luggage has been taken to your suite, Lady Rose. I'll take you through as soon as we're in the air,' Atiya said as she led her to an armchair-sized seat.

*A suite?*

Not *that* familiar, she thought, taking out her cellphone and sending a one word message to Rose to let her know that she'd got through security without any hiccups. Apart from Kalil al-Zaki, that was, and Rose couldn't do anything about that.

That done, she turned off the phone and looked around.

From the outside, apart from the royal livery, the aircraft might look much like any other. On the inside, however, it bore no similarity to the crammed-tight budget airlines that were a necessary evil to be endured whenever she wanted a week or two in the sun.

'Would you like something to drink before we take off?' Atiya asked.

Uh-oh.

*Take* and *off*, used in tandem, were her two least favourite words in the English language. Until now her head had been too busy concentrating on the role she was playing, enjoying the luxury of a chauffeur-driven limousine, free-wheeling around the unexpected appearance of Kalil al-Zaki, to confront that particular problem.

'Juice? A glass of water?'

'Water, thank you,' she replied, forcing herself to concentrate, doing her best not to look at the man who'd taken the seat across the aisle.

And failing.

His suit lay across his broad shoulders as if moulded to him and his glossy black hair, brushed back off a high forehead curled over his collar, softening features that could have been chiselled from marble. Apart from his mouth.

Marble could never do justice to the sensuous droop of a lower lip that evoked such an immediate, such a disturbing response in parts of her anatomy that had been dormant for so long that she'd forgotten how it felt.

As if sensing her gaze, Kalil al-Zaki turned and she blushed at being caught staring.

Nothing in his face suggested he had noticed. Instead, as the plane began to taxi towards the runway, he took an envelope from the inside pocket of his jacket and offered it to her.

'My introduction from Princess Lucy, Lady Rose.'

She accepted the square cream envelope, warm from his body, and although she formed the words, *Thank you*, no sound emerged. Praying that the dark pink net of her veil would camouflage the heat that had flooded into her cheeks, she ducked her head. It was embarrassment, she told herself as she flipped open the envelope and took out the note it contained.

*Dear Rose,*

*I didn't get a chance to call yesterday and explain that Han's cousin, Kalil al-Zaki, will be accompanying you to Bab el Sama.*

*I know that you are desperate to be on your own, but you will need someone to drive you, accompany you to the beach, be generally at your beck and call while you're in Bab el Sama and at least he won't report every move you make to your grandfather.*

*The alternative would be one of the Emir's guards, good men every one but, as you can imagine, not the most relaxing of companions.*

*Kal will not intrude if you decide to simply lie by the*

*pool with a book, but you shouldn't miss out on a visit to
the souk—it's an absolute treasure of gold, silks, spices—
or a drive into the desert. The peace is indescribable.*

*Do give me a call if there is anything you need or you
just need someone to talk to but, most of all rest, relax,
recharge the batteries and don't, whatever you do, give
Rupert a single thought.*

*All my love,*
*Lucy*

Which crushed her last desperate hope that he was simply
escorting her on the flight. 'There and back', apparently, included the seven days in between.

And things had been going so well up until now, she thought
as the stewardess returned with her water and she gratefully
gulped down a mouthful.

Too well.

Rose's grandfather had apparently accepted that taking her
own security people with her would be seen as an insult to her
hosts. The entire Ramal Hamrah ruling family had holiday
'cottages' at Bab el Sama and the Emir did not, she'd pointed
out, take the safety of his family or their guests lightly.

The paparazzi were going to have to work really hard to get
their photographs this week, although she'd do her best to
make it easy for them.

There had been speculation that Rupert would join Rose on
this pre-Christmas break and if she wasn't visible they might
just get suspicious, think they'd been given the slip. Raise a hue
and cry that would get everyone in a stew and blow her cover.

Her commission was to give them something to point their
lenses at so that the Duke was reassured that she was safe and
the world could see that she was where she was supposed to
be.

Neither of them had bargained on her friend complicating
matters.

Fortunately, Princess Lucy's note had made it clear that Rose hadn't met Kalil al-Zaki, which simplified things a little. The only question left was, faced with an unexpected—and unwanted—companion, what would Rose do now?

Actually, not something to unduly tax the mind. Rose would do what she always did. She'd smile, be charming, no matter what spanner had been thrown into her carefully arranged works.

Until now, protected by the aura of untouchability that seemed to encompass the Lady Rose image, Lydia had never had a problem doing the same.

But then spanners didn't usually come blessed with smooth olive skin moulded over bone structure that had been a gift from the gene fairies.

It should have made it easier to respond to his smile—if only with an idiotic, puppy-like grin. The reality was that she had to concentrate very hard to keep the drool in check, her hand from visibly trembling, her brain from turning to jelly. Speaking at the same time was asking rather a lot, but it certainly helped take her mind off the fact that the aircraft was taxiing slowly to the runway in preparation for the nasty business of launching her into thin air. She normally took something to calm her nerves before holiday flights but hadn't dared risk it today.

Fortunately, ten years of 'being' Lady Rose came to her rescue. The moves were so ingrained that they had become automatic and instinct kicked in and overrode the urge to leap into his lap and lick his face.

'It would seem that you've drawn the short straw, Mr al-Zaki,' she said, kicking the 'puppy' into touch and belatedly extending her hand across the aisle.

'The short straw?' he asked, taking it in his own firm grip with just the smallest hint of a frown.

'I imagine you have a dozen better things to do than…' she raised the letter an inch or two '…show me the sights.'

'On the contrary, madam,' he replied formally, 'I can assure you that I had to fight off the competition.'

He was so serious that for a moment he had her fooled. Unbelievable!

The man was flirting with her, or, rather, flirting with Lady Rose. What a nerve!

'It must have been a very gentlemanly affair,' she replied, matching his gravity, his formality.

One of his dark brows lifted the merest fraction and an entire squadron of butterflies took flight in her stomach. He was good. Really good. But any girl who'd worked for as long as she had on a supermarket checkout had not only heard it all, but had an arsenal of responses to put even the smoothest of operators in their place.

'No black eyes?' she prompted. 'No broken limbs?'

He wasn't quite quick enough to kill the surprise at the swiftness of her comeback and for a moment she thought she'd gone too far. He was the Ambassador's cousin, after all. One of the ruling class in a society where women were supposed to be neither seen nor heard.

Like that was going to happen...

But then the creases deepened in his cheeks, his mouth widened in a smile and something happened to the darkest, most intense eyes she'd ever seen. Almost, she thought, as if someone had lit a fire in their depths.

'I was the winner, madam,' he reminded her.

'I'm delighted you think so,' she replied, hanging on to her cool by the merest thread, despite the conflagration that threatened to ignite somewhere below her midriff.

There had never been anyone remotely like this standing at her supermarket checkout. She was going to have to be very, very careful.

Kal just about managed to bite back a laugh.

Lucy—with Hanif's unspoken blessing, he had no doubt—was placing him in front of the Emir, forcing his uncle to take note of his existence, acknowledge that he was doing something for his country. Offering him a chance to show himself to be someone worthy of trust, a credit to the name he was forbidden from using. And already he was flirting with the woman who had been entrusted to his care.

But then she wasn't the least bit what he'd expected.

He had seen a hundred photographs of Lady Rose on magazine covers and nothing in those images had enticed him to use her friendship with Princess Lucy to attempt a closer acquaintance.

The iconic blue eyes set in an oval face, yards of palest blonde hair, the slender figure were, no doubt, perfect. If you liked that kind of look, colouring, but she'd lacked the dark fire, a suggestion of dangerous passion, of mystery that he looked for in a woman.

The reality, he discovered, was something else.

As she'd walked into the VIP lounge it had seemed to come to life; as if, on a dull day, the sun had emerged from behind a cloud.

What he'd thought of as pallor was, in fact, light. A golden glow.

She was a lot more than a colourless clothes horse.

The famous eyes, secreted behind the wisp of veil that covered the upper half of her face, sparkled with an excitement, a vitality that didn't come through in any photograph he'd seen. But it was the impact of her unexpectedly full and enticingly kissable mouth, dark, sweet and luscious as the heart of a ripe fig, that grabbed and held his complete attention and had every red blood cell in his body bounding forward to take a closer look.

For the briefest moment her poise had wavered and she'd appeared as nonplussed as he was, but for a very different reason. It was obvious that Lucy hadn't managed to warn her that she was going to have company on this trip. She'd swiftly gathered herself, however, and he discovered that, along with all her other assets, she had a dry sense of humour.

Unexpected, it had slipped beneath his guard, and all his good intentions—to keep his distance, retain the necessary formality—had flown right out of the window.

And her cool response, 'I'm delighted you think so,' had

been so ambiguous that he hadn't the least idea whether she was amused by his familiarity or annoyed.

His life had involved one long succession of his father's wives and mistresses, a galaxy of sisters who ranged from nearly his own age to little girls. Without exception they were all, by turn, tempestuous, sphinxlike, teasing. He'd seen them in all their moods and it had been a very long time since he hadn't known exactly what a woman was thinking.

Now, while the only thought in his own head should be *danger, out of bounds,* what he really wanted was for her to lift that seductive little veil and, with that lovely mouth, invite him to be really bad…

Realising that he was still holding her hand, he made a determined effort to get a grip. 'You are as astute as you are lovely, madam,' he replied, matching her own cool formality, as he released it. 'I will be more circumspect in future.'

Her smile was a private thing. Not a muscle moved, only something in her eyes altered so subtly that he could not have described what happened. He'd felt rather than seen a change and yet he knew, deep down, that she was amused.

'Rose,' she said.

'I beg your pardon, madam?'

'According to her letter, Lucy thought you would make a more relaxing companion than one of the Emiri guard.'

'You have my word that I won't leap to attention whenever you speak to me,' he assured her.

'That is a relief, Mr al-Zaki.'

Lydia had to work a lot harder than usual to maintain the necessary regal poise.

She had no way of knowing on what scale Princess Lucy measured 'relaxing' but she must lead a very exciting life if spending time with Kalil al-Zaki fell into that category.

With his hot eyes turning her bones to putty, heating her skin from the inside out, *relaxed* was the last word she'd use to describe the way she was feeling right now.

'However, I don't find the prospect of an entire week being "madamed" much fun either. My name is...' she began confidently enough, but suddenly faltered. It was one thing acting out a role, it was quite another to look this man in the eye, meet his dark gaze and utter the lie. She didn't want to lie to him, to pretend... 'I would rather you called me Rose.'

'Rose,' he repeated softly. Wild honey...

'Can you manage your seat belt, Lady Rose?' the stewardess asked as she retrieved the glass. 'We're about to take off.'

'Oh...' Those words again. 'Yes, of course.'

She finally managed to tear her gaze away from her companion—wild honey was a dangerous temptation that could not be tasted without getting stung—and cast about her for the straps.

'Can I assist you, Rose?' he asked as her shaking hands fumbled with the buckle.

'No!' She shook her head as she finally managed to clip it into place. 'Thank you, Mr...'

'Kal,' he prompted. 'Most people call me Kal.' The lines bracketing his mouth deepened into a slow, sexy smile. 'When they're being relaxed,' he added.

She just about managed to stifle a hysterical giggle. She hadn't hesitated because she'd forgotten his name. He'd made an indelible impression...

No.

She'd been so busy worrying about whether he knew Rose personally, countering the effect of that seductive voice, that she'd overlooked the really important part of Princess Lucy's letter. The bit where she'd mentioned that Kalil al-Zaki was her husband's cousin. As she'd said the word 'Mr' it had suddenly occurred to her who he really was. Not just some minor diplomat who'd been given the task of ensuring a tricky visitor didn't get into trouble while she was at Bab el Sama.

Oh, dear me, no.

That wouldn't do for Lady Rose. Cousin of the Queen,

patron of dozens of charities as well as figurehead of the one
founded by her parents, she was an international figure and she
was being given the full red-carpet treatment. Right down to
her watchdog.

Kalil al-Zaki, the man who'd been roped in to guard their
precious guest, was the cousin of the Ambassador, Sheikh
Hanif al-Khatib. Which made him a nephew of the Emir
himself.

'Kal,' she squeaked, slamming her eyes closed and gripping
the arms of the chair as the plane rocketed down the runway
and the acceleration forced her back into the chair, for once in
her life grateful that she had her fear of take-off to distract her.

She was fine once she was in the air, flying straight and level
above the clouds with no horizon to remind her that she was
thirty thousand feet above the ground. Not that much different
from travelling on a bus, apart from the fact that you didn't have
to keep stopping so that people could get on and off.

Until now, what with one thing and another, she'd been
doing a better than average job of not thinking about this
moment, but not even the sudden realisation that Kalil al-Zaki
wasn't plain old *mister* anyone, but *Sheikh* Kalil al-Zaki, a
genuine, bona fide prince, could override her terror.

She'd have plenty of time to worry about how 'charming'
he'd prove to be if he discovered that she was a fake when they
were safely airborne.

But just when she'd reached the point where she forgot how
to breathe, long fingers closed reassuringly over hers and, surprised into sucking in air, she gasped and opened her eyes.

'I'm sorry,' Kal said as she turned to stare at him, 'but I've
never liked that bit much.'

What?

His expression was so grave that, for just a moment, she
wasn't sure whether or not he was serious. Then she swallowed.

Idiot.

Of course he wasn't serious. He was just being kind and, for once in her life, she wished she really was Lady Rose. Because then he'd be looking at her like that…

'You'll be all right now?' she managed, still breathless when, minutes later, the seat belt light pinged out. Doing her best to respond in kind, despite the fact that it was his steadying hand wrapped around hers. That she was the one who'd experienced a severe case of collywobbles. Wobbles that were still rippling through her, despite the fact that they had left the earth far beneath them.

'I believe so,' he replied gravely, but in no rush to break contact.

It was perhaps just as well that Atiya reappeared at that moment or they might have flown all the way to Ramal Hamrah with their hands intertwined.

Not that there would have been anything wrong with that…

'Shall I show you to your suite so that you can change before I serve afternoon tea, Lady Rose?'

'Thank you,' she said, using her traitorous hand to pull free the seat belt fastening so that she could follow Atiya. Straighten out her head.

Not easy when she discovered that the sumptuously fitted suite contained not only a bed, but its own bathroom with a shower that lent a whole new meaning to the words 'freshen up'.

'Would you like help changing?' Atiya offered, but Lydia assured her that she could manage and, once on her own, leaned back against the door, rubbing her palm over the hand Kal al-Zaki had held. Breathing slowly until her heart rate returned to normal. Or as near to normal as it was likely to be for the next week.

Kal watched Rose walk away from him.

His grandfather, a man who'd lost a throne, lost his country—but not the fortune that his father had hoped would compensate him for choosing his younger brother to succeed him—was a man without any purpose but to enjoy himself.

He'd become part of the jetset, a connoisseur of all things beautiful, including women.

Kalil's father had, as soon as he was old enough, taken the same path and Kalil too had come dangerously close to following in their footsteps.

His boyhood winters had been spent on the ski slopes of Gstaad and Aspen, his summers shared between an Italian palazzo and a villa in the South of France. He'd gone to school in England, university in Paris and Oxford, post-grad in America.

He had been brought up in an atmosphere of wealth and privilege, where nothing had been denied him. The female body held no mystery for him and hers, by his exacting standards, was too thin for true beauty.

So why did he find her finely boned ankles so enticing? What was it about the gentle sway of her hips that made his hand itch to reach out and trace the elegant curve from waist to knee? To undress her, slowly expose each inch of that almost translucent peaches and cream skin and then possess it.

Possess her.

'Can I fetch you anything, sir?' the stewardess asked as she returned.

Iced water. A cold shower...

He left it at the water but she returned empty-handed. 'Captain Jacobs sends his compliments and asked if you'd like to visit the flight deck, sir. I'll serve your water there,' she added, taking his acceptance for granted.

It was the very last thing he wanted to do, but it was a courtesy he could not refuse. And common sense told him that putting a little distance between himself and Rose while he cooled off would be wise.

He'd reached out instinctively when he'd seen her stiffen in fear as the plane had accelerated down the runway. It had been a mistake. Sitting beside her had been a mistake. His brief was to ensure her security and, despite Lucy's appeal to amuse her, distract her, make her laugh, that was it.

Holding her hand to distract her when she was rigid with fear didn't count, he told himself, but sitting here, waiting to see if he'd imagined his gut-deep reaction to her was not a good idea.

Especially when he already knew the answer.

Then the name registered. 'Jacobs? Would that be Mike Jacobs?'

'You are in so much trouble, Lydia Young.'

She hadn't underestimated the enormity of what she'd undertaken to do for Rose and they'd gone through every possible scenario, using a chat room to brainstorm any and all likely problems.

And every step of the way Rose had given her the opportunity to change her mind. Back out. Unfortunately, she was long past the *stop the plane, I want to get off* moment.

It had been too late from the moment she'd stepped out of that hotel room wearing Lady Rose's designer suit, her Jimmy Choos, the toes stuffed with tissue to stop them slipping.

Not that she would if she could, she realised.

She'd had ten years in which being 'Lady Rose' had provided all the little extras that helped make her mother's life easier. She *owed* Rose this. Was totally committed to seeing it through, but falling in lust at first sight with a man who had flirtation down to an art was, for sure, not going to make it any easier to ignore what Kalil al-Zaki's eyes, mouth, touch was doing to her.

'Come on, Lydie,' she said, giving herself a mental shake. 'You don't do this. You're immune, remember?'

Not since she'd got her fingers, and very nearly everything else, burnt by a stunningly good-looking actor who'd been paid to woo her into bed. She swallowed. She'd thought he was her Prince Charming, too.

It had been five years, but she still felt a cold shiver whenever she thought about it.

Pictures of the virginal 'Lady Rose' in bed with a man would have made millions for the people who'd set her up. Everyone would have run the pictures, whether they'd believed them or not. Covering themselves by the simple addition of a question mark to the 'Lady Rose in Sex Romp?' headline. The mere suggestion would have been enough to have people stampeding to the newsagents.

She, on the other hand, would have been ruined. No one would have believed she was an innocent dupe. If it had been anyone else, she wouldn't have believed it either.

She looked at the bed with longing, sorely tempted to just crawl beneath the covers and sleep away the next eight hours. No one would disturb her, expect anything from her.

But, since sleeping away the entire seven days was out of the question, she needed to snap out of it.

She'd been knocked off her feet by the heightened tension, that was all. Unsurprising under the circumstances. Anyone would be unsettled. Kal al-Zaki's presence had been unexpected, that was all. And she turned to the toilet case and overnight bag that had been placed on a stand.

The first was packed with everything a woman could ever need. The finest hairbrush that money could buy, the best skin care products, cosmetics, a selection of sumptuous scents; a perfect distraction for out of control hormones.

She opened one, sighed as she breathed in a subtle blend of sweet summer scents, then, as she sprayed it on her wrist, she caught an underlying note of something darker that tugged at forbidden desires. That echoed the heat in Kal al-Zaki's eyes.

Dropping it as if burned, she turned to the overnight bag. On the top, in suede drawstring bags, were the cases for the jewellery she was wearing, along with a selection of simpler pieces that Lady Rose wore while 'off duty'.

There was also a change of clothes for the long flight. A fine silk shirt the colour of champagne, wide-cut trousers in dark brown linen, a cashmere cardigan and a pair of butter-soft leather loafers in the right size. Supremely elegant but all wonderfully comfortable.

Rose had also packed a selection of the latest hardback bestsellers to while away the long flight. But then she hadn't expected that her stand-in would be provided with company.

Or not. According to Princess Lucy, it was up to her.

While she'd urged Rose to allow him to show her the sights, she'd made it clear that if she preferred to be alone then Kal would not intrude.

Not intrude?

What had the woman been *thinking?*

Hadn't she looked at him?

Anyone with half a brain could see that he wouldn't have to do a damn thing. One smile, one touch of his hand and he was already indelibly imprinted on her brain. In her head for ever more.

Intrusion squared.

In fact, if she didn't know better, she might be tempted to think that the Princess had planned a holiday romance as a little treat for her friend.

The idea was, of course, patently absurd.

Not that she didn't deserve a romance. A dark-eyed prince with a killer smile who'd sweep her off her feet.

No one deserved a little fun more than Rose, but anyone who knew her would understand just how impossible a casual, throwaway romance would be for her. And that was the essence of a holiday romance. Casual. Something out of time that had nothing to do with real life. That you left behind when you went home.

Anyone who truly cared for her would understand that.

Wouldn't they?

About to remove the pin that fastened the tiny hat to her chignon, she paused, sank onto the edge of the bed as a phrase in Lucy's letter came back to her.

*Don't give Rupert a single thought...*

She and Lucy were in total agreement on that one. Rose's

grandfather, the newspapers, even the masses out there who thought they knew her, might be clamouring for an engagement, but she'd seen the two of them together. There was absolutely no chemistry, no connection.

Rose had made a joke about it, but Lydia hadn't been fooled for a second. She'd seen the desperation in her face and anyone who truly cared for her would want to save her from sleepwalking into such a marriage simply because it suited so many people.

Could Princess Lucy have hoped that if she put Rose and Kalil together the sparks would fly of their own accord without any need to stoke the fire? No doubt about it, a week being flirted with by Kal al-Zaki would have been just the thing to bring the colour back into Rose's cheeks.

Or was it all less complicated than that?

Was Lucy simply relying on the ever-attendant paparazzi, seeing two young people alone in a perfect setting, to put one and one together and make it into a front page story that would make them a fortune?

Who cared whether it was true?

Excellent plan, Lucy, she thought, warming to the woman despite the problems she'd caused.

There was only one thing wrong with it. Lady Rose had taken matters into her own hands and was, even now—in borrowed clothes, a borrowed car—embarking on an adventure of her own, safe in the knowledge that no one realised she'd escaped. That she could do what she liked while the world watched her lookalike.

Of course there was nothing to stop her from making it happen, she thought as she finally removed the hat and jewellery she was wearing. Kicked off her shoes and slipped out of the suit.

All it would take would be a look. A touch. He wasn't averse to touching.

She began to pull pins from her hair, absently divesting herself of the Lady Rose persona, just as she did at the end of every gig.

And she wouldn't be the victim this time. She would be the one in control, watching as the biter was, for once, bit.

Then, as her hair tumbled down, bringing her out of a reverie in which Kal touched her hand, then her face, her neck, his lips following a trail blazed by his fingers she let slip a word that Rose had probably never heard, let alone used.

It had taken an age to put her hair up like that and, unlike Rose, she didn't have a maid to help.

Just what she deserved for letting her fantasy run away with her. There was no way she was going to do anything that would embarrass Rose. Her part was written and she'd stick to it.

She began to gather the pins, but then realised that just because Rose never appeared in photographs other than with her hair up, it didn't mean that when she shut the door on the world at the end of the day—or embarked on an eight-hour flight—she'd wouldn't wear it loose.

She was, after all, supposed to be on holiday. And who, after all, knew what she did, said, wore, when she was behind closed doors?

Not Kalil al-Zaki, that was for sure.

And that was the answer to the 'keeping up appearances' problem, she realised.

Instead of trying to remember that she was Lady Rose for the next seven days, she would just be herself. She'd already made a pretty good start with the kind of lippy responses that regulars on her checkout at the supermarket would recognise.

And being herself would help with the 'lust' problem, too.

For as long as she could remember, she'd been fending off the advances of first boys, then men who, when they looked at her, had seen only the 'virgin' princess and wanted to either worship or ravish her.

It had taken her a little while to work that one out but, once she had, she'd had no trouble keeping them at arm's length, apart from the near miss with the actor, but then he'd been paid to be convincing. And patient. It was a pity he'd only, in the end, had an audience of one because he'd put in an Oscar-winning performance.

Kal, despite the way he looked, was just another man flirting with Lady Rose. That was all she had to remember, she told herself as she shook out her hair, brushed it, before she freshened up and put on the clothes Rose had chosen for her.

So which would he be? Worshipper or ravisher?

Good question, she thought as she added a simple gold chain and stud earrings before checking her reflection in a full length mirror.

It wasn't quite her—she tended to favour jeans and funky tops. It wasn't quite Lady Rose either, but it was close enough for someone who'd never met either of them, she decided as she chose a book, faced the door and took a slow, calming breath before returning to the main cabin.

In her absence the seats had been turned around, the cabin reconfigured so that it now resembled a comfortable sitting room.

An empty sitting room.

# CHAPTER THREE

HAVING screwed herself up to be 'relaxed', the empty cabin was something of a let-down, but a table had been laid with a lace cloth and, no sooner than she'd settled herself and opened her book, Atiya arrived to serve afternoon tea.

Finger sandwiches, warm scones, clotted cream, tiny cakes and tea served from a heavy silver pot.

'Is all this just for me?' she asked when she poured only one cup and Kal had still not reappeared.

She hadn't wanted his company, but now he'd disappeared she felt affronted on Lady Rose's behalf. He was supposed to be here, keeping her safe from harm.

'Captain Jacobs invited Mr al-Zaki to visit the crew on the flight deck,' Atiya said. 'Apparently they did their basic training together.'

'Training?' It took her a moment. 'He's a *pilot*?'

Okay. She hadn't for a minute believed that he was bothered by the take-off, but she hadn't seen *that* coming. A suitable career for a nephew of an Emir wasn't a subject that had ever crossed her mind, but working as a commercial airline pilot wouldn't have been on her list even if she had. Maybe it had been military training.

A stint in one of the military academies favoured by royals would fit.

'Shall I ask him to rejoin you?' Atiya asked.

'No,' she said quickly. She had wanted him to keep his distance and her fairy godmother was, apparently, still on the case. 'I won't spoil his fun.'

Besides, if he returned she'd have to share this scrumptious spread.

Too nervous to eat lunch, and with the terrifying take-off well behind her, she was suddenly ravenous and the temptation to scoff the lot was almost overwhelming. Instead, since overindulgence would involve sweating it all off later, she managed to restrain herself, act like the lady she was supposed to be and simply tasted a little of everything to show her appreciation, concentrating on each stunning mouthful so that it felt as if she was eating far more, before settling down with her book.

Kal paused at the door to the saloon.

Rose, her hair a pale gold shimmer that she'd let down to hang over her shoulder, feet tucked up beneath her, absorbed in a book, was so far removed from her iconic image that she looked like a completely different woman.

Softer. The girl next door rather than a princess, because that was what she'd be if she'd been born into his culture.

Was the effect diminished?

Not one bit. It just came at him from a different direction. Now she looked not only luscious but available.

Double trouble.

As he settled in the chair opposite her she raised her eyes from her book, regarding him from beneath long lashes.

'Did you enjoy your visit to the cockpit?'

An almost imperceptible edge to her voice belied the softer look.

'It was most informative. Thank you,' he responded, equally cool. A little chill was just the thing to douse the heat generated by that mouth. Maybe.

'Did your old friend offer you the controls?' she added, as if reading his mind, and suddenly it all became clear. It wasn't the fact that he'd left her side without permission that bothered her.

The stewardess must have told her that he was a pilot and she thought he'd been laughing at her fear of flying.

'I hoped you wouldn't notice that little bump back there,' he said, offering her the chance to laugh right back at him.

There was a flicker of something deep in her eyes and the suspicion of an appreciative dimple appeared just above the left hand corner of her mouth.

'That was you? I thought it was turbulence.'

'Did you?' She was lying outrageously—the flight had been rock steady since they'd reached cruising altitude—but he was enjoying her teasing too much to be offended. 'It's been a while since I've flown anything this big. I'm a little rusty.'

She was struggling not to laugh now. 'It's not something you do seriously, then?'

'No one in my family does anything seriously.' It was the standard response, the one that journalists expected, and if it didn't apply to him, who actually cared? But, seeing a frown buckle the smooth, wide space between her eyes, the question that was forming, he cut her short with, 'My father bought himself a plane,' he said. 'I wanted to be able to fly it so I took lessons.'

'Oh.' The frown remained. 'But you said "this big",' she said, with a gesture that indicated the aircraft around them.

'You start small,' he confirmed. 'It's addictive, though. You keep wanting more.'

'But you've managed to break the habit.'

'Not entirely. Maybe you'd like a tour of the flight deck?' he asked. She clearly had no idea who he was and that suited him. If she discovered that he was the CEO of a major corporation she'd want to know what he was doing playing bodyguard. 'It sometimes helps ease the fear if you understand exactly what's happening. How things work.'

She shook her head. 'Thanks, but I'll pass.' Then, perhaps thinking she'd been less than gracious, she said, 'I do understand that my fear is totally irrational. If I didn't, I'd never get on one of these things.' Her smile was self-deprecating. 'But while, for the convenience of air travel, I can steel myself to suffer thirty seconds or so of blind panic, I also know that taking a pilot's eye view, seeing for myself exactly how much nothing there is out there, will only make things worse.'

'It's really just the take-off that bothers you?' he asked.

'So far,' she warned. 'But any attempt to analyse my fear is likely to give me ideas. And, before you say it, I know that flying is safer than crossing the road. That I've more chance of being hurt going to work—' She caught herself, for a fraction of second floundered. 'So I've heard,' she added quickly, as if he might dispute that what she did involved effort.

While opening the new wing of a hospital, attending charity lunches, appearing at the occasional gala might seem like a fairy tale existence to the outsider, he'd seen the effort Lucy put into her own charity and knew the appearance of effortless grace was all illusion.

But there was something about the way she'd stopped herself from saying more that suggested... He didn't know what it suggested.

'You've done your research.'

'No need. People will insist on telling you these things,' she said pointedly.

Signalling that the exchange was, as far as she was concerned, at an end, she returned to her book.

'There's just one more thing...'

She lifted her head, waited.

'I'm sure that Lucy explained that once we arrive in Ramal Hamrah we'll be travelling on to Bab el Sama by helicopter but—'

'Helicopter?'

The word came out as little more than a squeak.

'—but if it's going to be a problem, I could organise alternative transport,' he finished.

Lydia had been doing a pretty good job of keeping her cool, all things considered. She'd kept her head down, her nose firmly in her book even when Kal had settled himself opposite her. Stretched out those long, long legs. Crossed his ankles.

He'd removed his jacket, loosened his tie, undone the top button of his shirt.

What was it about a man's throat that was so enticing? she wondered. Invited touch...

She swallowed.

This was so not like her. She could flirt with the best, but that was no more than a verbal game that she could control. It was easy when only the brain was engaged...

*Concentrate!*

Stick to the plan. Speak when spoken to, keep the answers brief, don't let slip giveaways like 'going to work', for heaven's sake!

She'd managed to cover it but, unless she kept a firm rein on her tongue, sooner or later she'd say something that couldn't be explained away.

Lady Rose was charming but reserved, she reminded herself. *Reserved.*

She made a mental note of the word, underlined it for emphasis.

It was too late to recall the 'helicopter' squeak, however, and she experienced a hollow feeling that had nothing to do with hunger as Kal, suddenly thoughtful, said, 'You've never flown in one?'

*She* had never been in a helicopter, but it was perfectly possible that Lady Rose hopped about all over the place in one in order to fulfil her many engagements. Quite possibly with her good friend Princess Lucy.

She hadn't thought to ask. Why would she?

After what seemed like an eternity, when she was sure Kal was going to ask her what she'd done with the real Lady Rose, he said, 'So?'

'So?' she repeated hoarsely.

'Which is it to be?'

'Oh.' He was simply waiting for her to choose between an air-conditioned ride in leather-upholstered comfort, or a flight in a noisy machine that didn't even have proper wings. Her well-honed instinct for self-preservation was demanding she go for the four-wheeled comfort option.

Her mouth, taking no notice, said, 'I can live with the helicopter.'

And was rewarded with another of those smiles that bracketed his mouth, fanned around his eyes, as if he knew just how much it had cost her.

'It's certainly simpler,' he said, 'but if I get scared you will hold my hand, won't you?'

Lydia, jolted out of her determined reserve by his charm, laughed out loud. Then, when he didn't join in, she had the weirdest feeling that their entire conversation had been leading up to that question and it was her breath that momentarily caught in her throat.

'I don't believe you're scared of anything,' she said.

'Everyone is scared of something, Rose,' he said enigmatically as he stood up. 'I'll leave you to enjoy your book. If you need me for anything I'll be in the office.'

Showers, bedrooms, now an office…

'Please, don't let me keep you from your work,' she said.

'Work?'

He said the word lightly, as if it was something he'd never thought of, but a shadow, so brief that she might have missed it had she not been so intent on reading his thoughts, crossed his face and she felt horribly guilty at her lack of gratitude. No matter how inconvenient, this man, purely as a favour, had given up his own time to ensure she had the perfect holiday.

Or was he recalling her earlier slip?

'For the next seven days you are my first concern,' he assured her. 'I'm simply going to check the weather report.'

*Whew...*

His first concern.

*Wow...*

But then he thought that she was the real thing. And when he turned those midnight-dark eyes on her she so wanted to be real. Not pretending. Just for a week, she thought, as she watched him stride away across the cabin on long, long legs.

*No, no, no!*

This was no time to lose it over a gorgeous face and a buff body and, determined to put him out of her mind, she turned back to her book. She had to read the same paragraph four times before it made sense, but she persevered, scarcely wavering in her concentration even when Kal returned to his chair, this time armed with a book of his own.

She turned a page, taking the opportunity to raise her lashes just enough to see that it was a heavyweight political treatise. Not at all what she'd expect from a man with playboy looks who'd told her that he did nothing 'seriously'.

But then looks, as she knew better than most, could be deceptive.

Atiya appeared after a while with the dinner menu and to offer them a drink. They both stayed with water. Wasted no time in choosing something simple to eat.

But for the continuous drone of the aircraft engines, the cabin was quiet. Once she lifted her head, stretched her neck. Maybe the movement caught his eye because he looked up too, lifting a brow in silent query. She shook her head, leaned back against the thickly padded seat and looked down at a carpet of clouds silvered by moonlight.

Kal, watching her, saw the exact moment when her eyes closed, her body slackened and he caught her book as it began to slide from her hand. It was the autobiography of a woman who'd founded her own business empire. She'd personally inscribed this copy to Rose.

He closed it, put it on the table. Asked Atiya for a light

blanket, which he laid over her. Then, book forgotten, he sat and watched her sleep, wondering what dreams brought that tiny crease to her forehead.

'Sir,' Atiya said softly, 'I'll be serving dinner in ten minutes. Shall I wake Lady Rose?'

'I'll do it in a moment,' he said. Then, when she'd gone, he leaned forward. 'Rose,' he said softly. 'Rose…'

Lydia opened her eyes, for a moment not sure where she was. Then she saw Kal and it all came rushing back. It hadn't been a dream, then. She really was aboard a flying palace, one that wouldn't turn into a pumpkin at midnight. She had an entire week before she had to return to the checkout.

'What time is it?' she asked, sitting up, disentangling herself from the blanket that Atiya must have put over her.

'Seven minutes to eight in London, or to midnight in Ramal Hamrah if you want to set your watch to local time.'

She glanced at her wrist, touched the expensive watch, decided she'd rather do the maths than risk tampering with it.

'Atiya is ready to serve dinner.'

'Oh.' Her mouth was dry, a sure sign that she'd been sleeping with it open, which meant he'd been sitting there watching her drool.

Memo to self, she thought, wincing as she put her feet to the floor, searched with her toes for her shoes. Next time, use the bed.

'I apologise if I snored.'

His only response was a smile. She muffled a groan. She'd snored, drooled…

'Late night?' he asked, not helping.

'Very,' she admitted.

She'd had a late shift at the supermarket and, although her mother was determinedly independent, she always felt guilty about leaving her, even for a short time.

'I was double-checking to make sure that I hadn't left any loose ends trailing before taking off for a week,' she replied.

Everything clean and polished.

Fridge and freezer stocked so that Jennie wouldn't have to shop.

Enough of her mother's prescription meds to keep her going.

The list of contact numbers double-checked to make sure it was up to date.

While Rose wouldn't have been faced with that scenario, she'd doubtless had plenty of other stuff to keep her up late before she disappeared for a week.

And, like her, she would have been too wound up with nerves to sleep properly.

'I'd better go and freshen up,' she said but, before she could move, Kal was there to offer his hand, ease her effortlessly to her feet so that they were chest to chest, toe to toe, kissing close for a fraction of a second; long enough for her to breathe in the scent of freshly laundered linen, warm skin, some subtle scent that reminded her of a long ago walk in autumn woods. The crushed dry leaves and bracken underfoot.

Close enough to see the faint darkening of his chin and yearn to reach up, rub her hand over his jaw, feel the roughness against her palm.

She'd barely registered the thought before he released her hand, stepped back to let her move and she wasted no time putting some distance between them.

She looked a mess. Tousled, dishevelled, a red mark on her cheek where she'd slept with her head against the leather upholstery. She was going to have to duck her entire head under the cold tap to get it working properly, but she didn't have time for that. Instead, she splashed her face, repaired her lipstick, brushed the tangles out of her hair and then clasped it at the nape of her neck with a clip she found in the case that Rose had packed for her.

Then she ran through the pre-gig checklist in an attempt to jolt her brain back into the groove.

Smoothed a crease in the linen trousers.

Straightened the fine gold chain so that it lay in an orderly fashion about her neck.

Rehearsed her prompt list of appropriate questions so that there would never be a lull in the conversation.

Putting the situation in its proper context.

It was something she'd done hundreds of times, after all.

*It was just another job!*

Kal rose as she entered the main saloon and the *just another job* mantra went straight out of the window. Not that he *did* anything. Offer her his hand. Smile, even.

That was the problem. He didn't have to *do* anything, she thought as he stood aside so that she could lead the way to where Atiya was waiting beside a table that had been laid with white damask, heavy silver, crystal, then held a chair for her.

Like a force of nature, he just *was*.

Offered wine, she shook her head. Even if she'd been tempted, she needed to keep a clear head.

She took a fork, picked up a delicate morsel of fish and said, 'Lucy tells me that you're her husband's cousin. Are you a diplomat, too?'

Conventional, impersonal conversation. That was the ticket, she thought as she tasted the fish. Correction, ate the fish. She wasn't tasting a thing.

'No.' He shrugged. 'My branch of the family has been personae non gratae at the Ramal Hamrahn court for three generations.'

*No, no, no!*

That wasn't how it worked. She was supposed to ask a polite question. He was supposed to respond in kind. Like when you said, 'How are you?' and the only proper response was any variation on, 'Fine, thanks.'

'Personae non gratae at the Embassy, too,' he continued, 'until I became involved in one of Lucy's charitable missions.'

Better. Charity was Rose's life and, firmly quashing a desire to know more about the black sheep thing, what his family had done three generations ago that was so terrible—definitely off the polite questions list—Lydia concentrated on that.

'You help Lucy?'

'She hasn't mentioned what I do?' he countered.

'Maybe she thought I'd try and poach you.' Now that was *good.* 'What do you do for her?'

'Not much. She needed to ship aid to an earthquake zone. I offered her the use of an aircraft—we took it from there.'

Very impressively 'not much', she thought. She'd definitely mention him to Rose. Maybe they would hit it off.

She squashed down the little curl of something green that tried to escape her chest.

'That would be the one your father owns?' she asked. Again, she'd imagined a small executive jet. Clearly, where this family was concerned, she needed to start thinking bigger.

'Flying is like driving, Rose. When you get your licence, you don't want to borrow your father's old crate. You want a shiny new one of your own.'

'You do?'

A lot bigger, she thought. He came from a two-plane family. Something else occurred to her.

He'd said no one in his family did anything seriously, but that couldn't possibly be true. Not in his case, anyway. Obtaining a basic pilot's licence was not much different from getting a driving licence—apart from the cost—but stepping up to this level took more than money. It took brains, dedication, a great deal of hard work.

And, yes, a heck of a lot of money.

'You are such a fraud,' she said but, far from annoying her, it eased her qualms about her own pretence.

'Fraud?'

Kal paused with a fork halfway to his lips. It hadn't taken Lucy ten minutes to rumble him, demand to know what he expected from Hanif in return for his help, but she knew the family history and he hadn't expected his offer to be greeted with open arms.

He'd known the only response was to be absolutely honest with her. That had earned him first her sympathy and then, over the years, both her and Hanif's friendship.

Rose had acted as if she had never heard of him but, unless Lucy had told her, how did she—

'Not serious?' she prompted. 'Exactly how long did it take you to qualify to fly something like this?'

Oh, right. She was still talking about the flying. 'I do fun seriously,' he said.

'Fun?'

'Give me a chance and I'll show you,' he said. Teasing was, after all, a two-way street; the only difference between them was that she blushed. Then, realising how that might have sounded, he very nearly blushed himself. 'I didn't mean... Lucy suggested you might like to go fishing.'

'Fishing?' She pretended to consider. 'Let me see. Wet. Smelly. Maggots. That's your idea of fun?'

That was a challenge if ever he'd heard one. And one he was happy to accept. 'Wet, smelly and then you get to dry out, get warm while you barbecue the catch on the beach.'

'Wet, smelly, smoky and then we get sand in our food. Perfect,' she said, but a tiny twitch at the corner of her mouth suggested that she was hooked and, content, he let it lie.

Rose speared another forkful of fish.

'In her letter,' she said, 'Lucy suggested I'd enjoy a trip to the souk. Silk. Spices. Gold.'

'Heat, crowds, people with cellphones taking your photograph? I thought you wanted peace and privacy.'

'Even the paparazzi have children to feed and educate,' she said. 'And publicity oils the wheels of charity. The secret is not to give them something so sensational that they don't have to keep coming back for more.'

'That makes for a very dull life,' he replied gravely, playing along, despite the fact that it appeared to fly directly in the face of what Lucy had told him. 'But if you wore an *abbayah,* kept your eyes down, your hair covered, you might pass unnoticed.'

'A disguise?'

'More a cover-up. There's no reason to make it easy for them, although there's no hiding your height.'

'Don't worry about it.'

'It's what I'm here for.'

'Really?' And she was the one challenging him, as if she knew he had an agenda of his own. But she didn't wait for an answer. 'So what did you buy?' she asked.

He must have looked confused because she added, 'Car, not plane. I wouldn't know one plane from another. When you passed your test?' she prompted. 'A Ferrari? Porsche?'

'Far too obvious. I chose a Morgan.'

Her turn to look puzzled.

'It's a small sports car. A roadster,' he explained, surprised she didn't know that. 'The kind of thing that you see pilots driving in old World War Two movies? My father put my name on the waiting list on my twelfth birthday.'

'There's a waiting list?'

'A long one. They're hand-built,' he replied, smiling at her astonishment. 'I took delivery on my seventeenth birthday.'

'I'll add patient to serious,' she replied. 'What do you drive now?'

'I still have the Morgan.'

'The same one?'

'I'd have to wait a while for another one, so I've taken very good care of it.'

'I'm impressed.'

'Don't be. It stays in London while I'm constantly on the move, but for the record I drive a Renault in France, a Lancia in Italy and in New York…' he grinned '…I take a cab.'

'And in Ramal Hamrah?' she asked.

Suddenly the smile took real effort.

'There's an old Land Rover that does the job. What about you?' he asked, determined to shift the focus of their conversation to her. 'What do you drive for pleasure?'

She leaned forward, her lips parted on what he was sure would have been a protest that she wasn't finished with the question of Ramal Hamrah. Maybe something in his expression warned her that she was treading on dangerous ground and, after a moment, she sat back. Thought about it.

He assumed that was because her grandfather's garage offered so wide a choice. But then she said, 'It's...' she used her hands to describe a shape '...red.'

'Red?' Why was he surprised? 'Good choice.'

'I'm glad you approve.'

The exchange was, on the surface, perfectly serious and yet the air was suddenly bubbling with laughter.

'Do you really have homes in all those places?' she asked.

'Just a mews cottage in London. My mother, my father's first wife, was a French actress. She has a house in Nice and an apartment in Paris. His second wife, an English aristocrat, lives in Belgravia and Gloucestershire. His third was an American heiress. She has an apartment in the Dakota Building in New York and a house in the Hamptons.'

'An expensive hobby, getting married.' Then, when he made no comment, 'You stay with them? Even your ex-stepmothers?'

'Naturally. They're a big part of my life and I like to spend time with my brothers and sisters.'

'Oh, yes. I didn't think...' She seemed slightly flustered by his father's admittedly louche lifestyle. 'So where does Italy come in? The Lancia?' she prompted.

'My father bought a palazzo in Portofino when he was wooing a contessa. It didn't last—she quickly realised that he wasn't a man for the long haul—but he decided to keep the house. As he said, when a man has as many ex-wives and mistresses and children as he has, he needs a bolt-hole. Not true, of course. It's far too tempting a location. He's never alone.'

He expected her to laugh. Most people took what he said at face value, seeing only the glamour.

'From his history, I'd say he's never wanted to be,' Rose

said, her smile touched with compassion. 'It must have been difficult. Growing up.'

'Life was never dull,' he admitted with rather more flippancy than he felt. Without a country, a purpose, his grandfather had become rudderless, a glamorous playboy to whom women flocked, a lifestyle that his father had embraced without question. His family were his world but after one relationship that had kept the gossip magazines on their toes for eighteen months as they'd followed every date, every break up, every make up, he'd realised that he had no wish to live like that for the rest of his life.

'You didn't mention Ramal Hamrah,' she said, ignoring the opportunity he'd given her to talk about her own grandfather. Her own life.

Rare in a woman.

Rare in anyone.

Most people would rather talk about themselves.

'Do you have a home there?'

'There is a place that was once home,' he told her because the apartment overlooking the old harbour, bought off plan from a developer who had never heard of Kalil al-Zaki, could never be described as the home of his heart, his soul. 'A faded photograph that hangs upon my grandfather's wall. A place of stories of the raids, battles, celebrations that are the history of my family.'

Stories that had grown with the telling until they had become the stuff of legend.

It was an image that the old man looked at with longing. Where he wanted to breathe his last. Where he wanted to lie for eternity, at one with the land he'd fought for.

And Kalil would do anything to make that possible. Not that sitting here, sharing a meal with Lady Rose Napier was as tedious as he'd imagined it would be.

'No one has lived there for a long time,' he said.

For a moment he thought she was going to ask him to tell her more, but all she said was, 'I'm sorry.'

She was quiet for a moment, as if she understood the emptiness, the sense of loss and he began to see why people, even those who had never met her, instinctively loved her.

She had an innate sensitivity. A face that invited confidences. Another second and he would have told her everything but, at exactly the right moment, she said, 'Tell me about your brothers and sisters.'

'How long have you got?' he asked, not sure whether he was relieved or disappointed. 'I have one sister, a year younger than me. I have five half-sisters, three half-brothers and six, no seven, steps of both sexes and half a dozen who aren't actually related by blood but are still family.'

She counted them on her long, slender fingers.

'Sixteen?' she asked, looking at him in amazement. 'You've got sixteen brothers and sisters? Plus six.'

'At the last count. Sarah, she's the English ex, and her husband are about to have another baby.'

Lydia sat back in her chair, stunned. As an only child she had dreamed of brothers and sisters, but this was beyond imagining.

'Can you remember all their names?' she asked.

'Of course. They are my family.' Then, seeing her doubt, he held up his hand and began to list them. 'My sister is Adele. She's married to a doctor, Michel, and they have two children, Albert and Nicole. My mother has two other daughters by her second husband…'

As they ate, Kal talked about his family in France, in England and America. Their partners and children. The three youngest girls whose mothers his father had never actually got around to marrying but were all part of a huge extended family. All undoubtedly adored.

His family, but nothing about himself, she realised. Nothing about his personal life and she didn't press him. How a man talked about his family said a lot about him. She didn't need anyone to tell her that he was a loyal and caring son. That he loved his family. It was there in his smile as he told stories about his mother in full drama queen mode, about his sister. His pride in all their achievements.

If he'd had a wife or partner, children of his own, he would certainly have talked about them, too. With love and pride.

'You're so lucky having a big family,' she told him as they laughed at a story about one of the boys causing mayhem at a party.

'That's not the half of it,' he assured her. 'My grandfather set the standard. Five wives, ten children. Do you want their names, too? Or shall I save that for a rainy day?'

'Please tell me that it doesn't rain in Ramal Hamrah.'

'Not often,' he admitted.

Neither of them said anything while Atiya cleared the table, placed a tray of sweet things, tiny cakes, nuts, fruit, before them.

'Can I bring you coffee or tea?' Atiya asked.

'Try some traditional mint tea,' Kal suggested before she could reply. He spoke to Atiya in Arabic and, after a swift exchange, which apparently elicited the right answer, he said, 'Not made with a bag, it will be the real thing.'

'It sounds delicious.'

'It is.'

He indicated the tray, but she shook her head.

'It all looks wonderful but I can't eat another thing,' Lydia said. 'I hope there's a pool in Bab el Sama. If I keep eating like this I won't fit into any of my clothes when I get home.'

'I don't understand why women obsess about being thin,' he said.

'No? Have you never noticed the way celebrities who put on a few pounds are ridiculed? That would be women celebrities,' she added.

'I know. Adele went through a bad patch when she was a teenager.' He shook his head. Took a date, but made no attempt to push her to eat. Instead, he bestowed a lazy smile on her and said, 'Now you know my entire family. Your turn to tell me about yours.'

Lydia waited while Atiya served the mint tea.

Completely absorbed by his complex relationships, the little vignettes of each of his brothers and sisters that had made them all seem so real, she had totally forgotten the pretence and needed a moment to gather herself.

'Everyone knows my story, Kal.'

Kal wondered. While he'd been telling her about his family, she'd been by turns interested, astonished, amused. But the moment he'd mentioned hers, it was as if the lights had dimmed.

'I know what the press write about you,' he said. 'What Lucy has told me.'

That both her parents had been killed when she was six years old and she'd been raised by an obsessively controlling grandfather, the one who'd taken a newspaper headline literally and turned her into the 'people's angel'.

'What you see is what you get,' she replied, picking up the glass of tea.

Was it?

It was true that with her pale hair, porcelain skin and dazzling blue eyes she could have stepped out of a Renaissance painting.

But then there was that mouth. The full sultry lips that clung for a moment to the small glass as she tasted the tea.

A tiny piece of the crushed leaf clung to her lower lip and, as she gathered it in with the tip of her tongue, savouring the taste, he discovered that he couldn't breathe.

'It's sweet,' she said.

'Is that a problem?'

She shook her head. 'I don't usually put sugar in mint tea, but it's good.' She finished the tea, then caught at a yawn that, had she been anyone else, he would have sworn was fake. That she was simply making an excuse to get away. 'If you'll excuse me, Kal, it's been a long day and I'd like to try and get a couple of hours' sleep before we land.'

'Of course,' he said, easing her chair back so that she could stand up and walking with her to the door of her suite, unable to quite shake the feeling that she was bolting from the risk that he might expect the exposure of her own family in return for his unaccustomed openness.

Much as he adored them, he rarely talked about his family to outsiders. He'd learned very early how even the most innocent remark to a friend would be passed on to their parents and, in a very short time, would appear in print, twisted out of recognition by people who made a living out of celebrity gossip.

Rose, though, had that rare gift for asking the right question, then listening to the answer in a way that made a man feel that it was the most important thing she'd ever heard.

But then, at the door, she confounded him, turning to face him and, for a moment, locked in that small, still bubble that enclosed two people who'd spent an evening together, all the more intimate because of their isolation as they flew high above the earth in their own small time capsule, neither of them moved and he knew that if she'd been any other woman, if he'd been any other man, he would have kissed her. That she would have kissed him back. Maybe done a lot more than kiss.

She was a warm, quick-witted, complex woman and there had, undoubtedly, been a connection between them, a spark that in another world might have been fanned into a flame.

But she was Lady Roseanne Napier, the 'people's angel'. And he had made a promise to his grandfather that nothing, no one, would divert him from keeping.

'Thank you for your company, Rose,' he said, taking her hand and lifting it to his lips, but his throat was unexpectedly constricted as he took a step back. He added, 'Sleep well.'

It was going to be a very long week.

# CHAPTER FOUR

TIRED as she was, Lydia didn't sleep. Eyes closed, eyes open, it made no difference.

The hand Kal had kissed lay on the cover at her side and she had to press it down hard to keep it from flying to her mouth so that she could taste it.

Taste him.

His mouth had barely made contact and yet the back of her fingers throbbed as if burned, her body as fired up as if she'd had a faint electric shock.

In desperation she flung herself off the bed, tore off her clothes and threw herself beneath the shower, soaping herself with a gel that smelled faintly of lemons. Warm at first, then cooler until she was shivering. But still her skin burned and when Lydia lifted her hand to her face, breathed in, it was not the scent of lemons that filled her head.

It was nothing as simple as scent, but a distillation of every look, every word, the food they'd eaten, the mint tea they'd drunk. It had stirred the air as he'd bent over her hand, leaving her faint with the intensity of pure sensation that had rippled through her body. Familiar and yet utterly unknown. Fire and ice. Remembered pleasure and the certainty of pain.

Distraction.

She needed a distraction, she thought desperately as she wrapped herself in a fluffy gown, combed out her damp hair, applied a little of some unbelievably expensive moisturiser in an attempt to counteract the drying effects of pressured air.

She could usually lose herself in a book—she'd managed it earlier, even dozed off—but she'd left her book in the main cabin and nothing on earth would tempt her back out there until she had restored some semblance of calm order to her racketing hormones.

She chose another book from the selection Rose had packed for her and settled back against the pillows. All she had to do now was concentrate. It shouldn't be hard, the book was by a favourite author, but the words refused to stay still.

Instead they kept merging into the shape of Kal's mouth, the sensuous curve of his lower lip.

'Get a grip, Lydie!' she moaned, abandoning the book and sliding down to the floor where she sat cross-legged, hoping that yoga breathing would instil a modicum of calm, bring her down from what had to be some kind of high induced by an excess of pheromones leaking into the closed atmosphere of the aircraft.

Combined with the adrenalin charge of confronting the newsmen, tension at the prospect of facing airport security with Rose's passport, then the shock of Kalil al-Zaki arriving to mess up all their carefully laid plans, it was scarcely any wonder that the words wouldn't stay still.

That he was astoundingly attractive, took his duty of care to extraordinary lengths, had flirted outrageously with her hadn't helped.

When they'd sat down to their dinner party in the sky, she'd been determined to keep conversation on the impersonal level she employed at cocktail parties, launches.

Kal had blown that one right out of the water with his reply to her first question and she'd forgotten all about the 'plan' as he'd in turn amused, shocked, delighted her with tales of his family life.

And made her envious at the obvious warmth and affection they shared. His might be a somewhat chaotic and infinitely extendable family but, as an only child with scarcely any close relations, she'd been drawn in by the charm of having so many people who were connected to you. To care for and who cared back. Who would not want to be part of that?

And that was only half the story, she realised. Sheikh Hanif was his cousin and there must be a vast Ramal Hamrahn family that he hadn't even mentioned, other than to tell her that he and his family were personae non gratae at the Ramal Hamrahn court.

More, she suspected, than he told most people. But then Rose had that effect on people. Drew them out.

Instead, he had turned the spotlight on her, which was when she'd decided to play safe and retire.

There was a tap on the door. 'Madam? We'll be landing in fifteen minutes.'

'Thank you, Atiya.'

She reapplied a light coating of make-up. Rose might want her picture in the paper, but not looking as if she'd just rolled out of bed. Brushed out her hair. Dressed. Putting herself back together so that she was fit to be seen in public.

The seat belt sign pinged as she returned to the cabin and she shook her head as Kal half rose, waved him back to his seat and sat down, fastening her seat belt without incident before placing her hands out of reach in her lap. Not looking at him, but instead peering out at the skein of lights skirting the coast, shimmering in the water below them.

'Landing holds no terrors for you?' Kal asked and she turned to glance at him. A mistake. Groomed to perfection he was unforgettable, but after eight hours in the air, minus his tie, in need of a shave, he was everything a woman would hope to wake up to. Sexily rumpled, with eyes that weren't so much come to bed, as let's stay here for the rest of the day.

As if she'd know…

Quickly turning back to the window as they sank lower and the capital, Rumaillah, resolved from a mass of lights into individual streets, buildings, her attention was caught by a vast complex dominated by floodlit domes, protected by high walls, spread across the highest point of the city.

'What is that?' she asked.

Kal put a hand on the arm of her chair and leaned across so that he could see out of her window, but he must have dialled down the pheromone count, or maybe, like her, he was tired because, even this close, there was no whoosh of heat.

'It's the Emiri Palace,' he told her.

'But it's huge.'

'It's not like Buckingham Palace,' he said, 'with everything under one roof. The Emir's palace is not just one building. There are gardens, palaces for his wives, his children and their families. The Emiri offices are there too, and his Majlis where his people can go and see him, talk to him, ask for his help, or to intercede in disputes.'

'I like the sound of that. The man at the top being approachable.'

'I doubt it's quite as basic as it was in the old days,' he replied. There was an edge to his voice that made her forget about the exotic hilltop palace and look more closely at him. 'We've come a long way from a tent in the desert.'

We.

He might be excluded but he still thought of himself as one of them. She resisted the urge to ask him. If he wanted her to know he would tell her.

But, fascinated, she pressed, 'In theory, anyone can approach him?'

'In theory.'

There was something in his voice, a tension, anger, that stopped her from saying more.

'And you said "wives". How many has he got?'

'The Emir? Just one. The tradition of taking more than one wife began when a man would take the widows, children of brothers slain in battle into his family. Then it became a sign of wealth. It's rare these days.' Then, with a curl of his lip that could have been mistaken for a smile if you hadn't seen the real thing, 'My family are not typical.'

'And even they take only one at a time,' she replied, lifting her voice a little so that it was gently teasing.

'Legally,' he agreed. 'In practice there tends to be some overlap.'

'And you, Kal?'

'How many wives do I have?' And this time the smile was a little less forced. 'None, but then I'm a late starter.'

That she doubted, but suddenly the runway lights were whizzing past and then they were down with barely a bump.

Before she left the aircraft she visited the cockpit—now that it was safely on the ground—to thank the crew for a wonderful flight and, by the time she stepped outside into the warm moist air of the Gulf, her luggage had already been transferred to the waiting helicopter.

'Ready?' Kal asked.

She swallowed, nodded.

She'd been bold enough when the reality of committing her safety to what seemed to be a very small, fragile thing beside the bulk of the jet had been a distant eight hours away.

Now she was afraid that if she opened her mouth her teeth would start chattering like a pair of castanets.

Apparently she wasn't fooling Kal because he said, 'That ready? It's not too late to change your mind.'

She refused to be so pathetic and, shaking her head once in a *let's get this over with* gesture, she took a determined step forward. His hand at her back helped keep her moving when she faltered. Got her through the door and into her seat.

He said something to the pilot as he followed her—what, she couldn't hear above the noise of the engine.

He didn't bother to ask if she needed help with the straps, but took them from her and deftly fastened them as if it was something he'd been doing all his life. Maybe he had.

Then he gently lowered the earphones that would keep out

the noise and allow the pilot to talk to them onto her head, settling them into place against her ears.

'Okay?' he said, not that she could hear, but she'd been sent on a lip-reading and signing course by the supermarket and had no problem understanding him.

She nodded and he swiftly dealt with his own straps and headset before turning in his seat so that he was facing her.

'Hands,' he said, and when she lifted them to look at them, not knowing what she was supposed to do with them, he took them in his and held them as the rotor speed built up.

She tried to smile but this was far worse than in a passenger aircraft. Everything—the tarmac, the controls, the reality of what was happening—was so close, so immediate, so in your face.

There was no possibility of pretence here.

No way you could tell yourself that you were on the number seven bus going to work and, as the helicopter lifted from the ground, leaving her stomach behind, she tightened her grip of his hands but, before the scream bubbling up in her throat could escape, Kal leaned forward and said, 'Trust me, Rose.'

And then he kissed her.

It wasn't a gentle kiss. It was powerful, strong, demanding her total attention and the soaring lift as they rose into the air, leaving the earth far behind them, was echoed by a rush of pure exhilaration that flooded through her.

This was flying. This was living. And, without a thought for what would follow, she kissed him back.

Kal had seen Rose's momentary loss of courage as she'd looked across the tarmac from the top of the aircraft steps to the waiting helicopter, followed by the lift of her chin, an unexpectedly stubborn look that no photographer had ever managed to capture, as she'd refused to back down, switch to the car.

It didn't quite go with the picture Lucy had painted of the gentle, biddable girl—woman—who'd lovingly bowed to the dictates of her grandfather. Who was desperate for some quiet time while she fathomed out her future.

That was a chin that took no prisoners and, certain that once she was airborne she'd be fine, he hadn't argued. Even so, her steps had faltered as they'd neared the helicopter and as they'd boarded he'd told the pilot to get a move on before she had time for second thoughts.

This was not a moment for the usual round of 'Lady Rose' politeness, handshakes, introductions. All that could wait until they arrived at Bab el Sama.

And he'd done his best to keep her distracted, busy, her eyes on him rather than the tarmac.

But as the engine note changed in the moment prior to take-off, her hands had gripped his so hard that her nails had dug into his palms and he thought that he'd completely misjudged the situation, that she was going to lose it.

Hysterics required more than a reassuring hand or smile, they needed direct action and there were just two options—a slap or a kiss.

No contest.

Apart from the fact that the idea of hitting anyone, let alone a frightened woman, was totally abhorrent to him, letting go of her hands wasn't an option.

His 'Trust me' had been a waste of breath—she couldn't hear him—but it had made him feel better as he went in for the kiss, hard and fast. This wasn't seduction, this was survival and he wanted her total attention, every emotion, fixed on him, even if that emotion was outrage.

He didn't get outrage.

For a moment there was nothing. Only a stunned stillness. Then something like an imperceptible sigh breathed against his mouth as her eyes closed, the tension left her body and her lips softened, yielded and clung to his for a moment, warm and sweet as a girl's first kiss. Then parted, hot as a fallen angel tempting him to sin.

At which point the only one in danger of losing anything was him.

How long was a kiss? A heartbeat, minutes, a lifetime?

It seemed like all three as his hands, no longer captive, moved to her waist, her back, drawing her closer. A heartbeat while he breathed in the clean, fresh scent of her skin; minutes as the kiss deepened and something darker, more compelling stirred his senses; a lifetime while his hormones stampeded to fling themselves into the unknown without as much as a thought for the consequences.

Exactly like his grandfather. Exactly like his father.

Men without a purpose, without a compass, who'd put their own selfish desires above everything.

That thought, like a pitcher of cold water, was enough to jar him back to reality, remind him why he was here, and he drew back.

Rose took a gasping, thready little breath as he broke the connection. Sat unmoving for long moments before her lids slowly rose, almost as if the long, silky lashes were too heavy to lift.

Her lips parted as if she was going to speak but she closed them again without saying a word, instead concentrating on her breathing, slowing it down using some technique that she'd probably learned long ago to manage nerves.

When she raised her lashes again, she was sufficiently in control to speak.

He couldn't hear what she was saying, but she mouthed the words so carefully that he could lip-read enough to get the gist, which was, as near as damn it, 'If you were that scared, Kal, you should have told me. We could have taken the car.'

It was the response of a woman who, with ten years of interaction with the public behind her, knew exactly how to rescue an awkward moment, who could put anyone at ease with a word.

It put a kiss that had spiralled out of hand into perspective, allowing them both to move on, forget it.

Well, what had he expected?

That she'd fall apart simply because he'd kissed her?

She might—or might not—be a virgin princess, but she'd already proved, with her dry and ready wit, that she was no shrinking violet.

He knew he should be grateful that his rescue mission had been recognised for what it was. Received with her legendary good humour, charm.

But he wasn't grateful. Didn't want to forget.

He wanted to pull her close, kiss her again until that classy English cool sizzled away to nothing, her 'charm' shattered in a pyrotechnic blaze that would light up the night sky and this tender Rose, nurtured under glass, broke out and ran wild.

It wasn't going to happen.

Even if had been an appropriate time or place, their destinies were written. Even if she rejected the Earl in waiting her grandfather had lined up to walk her down the aisle and chose someone for herself, it was never going to be the scion of a disgraced and dispossessed exile.

And when he took a bride, it would not be in response to carnal attraction, the sexual chemistry that masqueraded as love, stealing your senses, stealing your life. His marriage would be an affair of state that would cement an alliance with one of the great Ramal Hamrahn families— the Kassimi, the Attiyah or the Darwish. The surrender of one of their precious daughters an affirmation that he had restored his family to their rightful place.

Had brought his grandfather home.

But time was running out. He had been infinitely patient and he no longer had years. His grandfather was already on borrowed time, stubbornly refusing to accept the death sentence that had been passed on him until he saw his grandson married as a Khatib should be married. Could die in peace in the place where he'd been born.

An affair that would cause scandalised headlines worldwide would do nothing to help his cause. He had to keep himself focused on what was important, he reminded himself, even while he held Rose, could feel her corn silk hair tumbling over his hands, her soft breath upon his cheek.

Fight, as he'd always fought, the demanding, selfish little gene he'd inherited, the one telling him to go for it and hang the consequences. The knowledge that she wanted it as much as he did. The pretence that it would just be a holiday romance, wouldn't hurt anyone.

That wasn't true. You could not give that much and walk away without losing something of yourself, taking something of the other with you. Already, in the closeness of the hours they had spent together, he had given more than he should. Had taken more. He concentrated on the clean, vast infinity of the night sky—diamonds against black velvet—until it filled his head, obliterating everything else.

Lydia wanted to curl up and die with embarrassment. Not because Kal had kissed her. That had been no more than straightforward shock tactics, designed to prevent her from doing something stupid.

And it had worked.

She hadn't screamed, hadn't tried to grab the pilot and make him stop.

Why would she when the minute his lower lip had touched hers, she'd forgotten all about the fact that they were rising from the ground in a tiny glass bubble?

Forgotten her fear.

Forgotten everything as the warmth of his mouth had first heated her lips, then curled through every part of her body, touching the frozen core that had remained walled up, out of reach for so long. As it felt the warmth, whimpered to be set free, he'd drawn her close and the kiss had ceased to be shock tactics and had become real, intense.

A lover's kiss, and as her arms had wrapped themselves around his neck she hadn't cared who he thought she was. He was kissing her as if he wanted her and that was all that mattered, because she wanted him right back.

She hadn't cared that he thought it was Rose who'd reacted so wantonly. Who'd wanted more. Who would still be kissing him as if the world was about to end if he hadn't backed off.

He was still holding her, still close enough that she could feel him breathing. Close enough that when she was finally brave enough to open her eyes she could see the *what-the-hell-happened-there?* look in his eyes. She wanted to explain that it was okay. That she wasn't Rose, just some dumb idiot girl who was having a very strange day.

That he could forget all about it. Forget about her.

But that was impossible.

She had to put things right, restore Rose's reputation. Instead, she closed her eyes again and concentrated on her breathing. Slowing it down. And, as her mind cleared, she realised that the answer was simple. Fear.

She could put it all down to her fear. Or his, she thought, remembering how he'd pretended to be the one who was scared as they'd lifted off.

If she could make him laugh it would be all right. They would be able to move on, pretend it had never happened.

But he hadn't laughed; there was no reaction at all and she realised that just because she could lip-read didn't mean that he could, too. He hadn't a clue what she was saying.

She took her hands from his shoulders, tried to concentrate on what he was saying as he looked up, beyond her. Shook her head to indicate that it hadn't got through.

He turned, looked straight at her as he repeated himself. 'And miss this?'

What?

She didn't want to take her eyes from him. While she was looking at him, while he was still holding her, she could forget that there was nothing but a thin wall of perspex between her and the sky.

But he lifted one of his dark brows a fraction of a millimetre, challenging her to be brave, and she finally tore her gaze from him, turned her head.

In the bubble of the helicopter they had an all round view of the sky which, away from the light pollution of the airport, the city, she could see as it was meant to be seen, with the constellations diamond-bright, the spangled shawl of the Milky Way spread across the heavens.

It was an awe-inspiring, terrifying sight. A reminder of how small they were. How vulnerable. And yet how spectacularly amazing and she didn't look away. But, although she wanted to reach back, share the moment with Kal, she remembered who she was supposed to be.

Not the woman on the checkout who anyone could—and did—flirt with. Not Lydia Young, who had a real problem with leaving the ground, but Lady Rose Napier, who could handle an unexpected kiss with the same natural charm as any other minor wobble in her day.

Instead, she concentrated on this unexpected gift he'd given her, searching for constellations that she recognised until she had to blink rather hard because her eyes were watering. At the beauty of the sky. That was all…

Kal must have said something. She didn't hear him, just felt his breath against her cheek, then, as he pointed down, she saw a scatter of lights below, the navigation lights of boats riding at anchor as they crossed a wide creek.

As they dropped lower, circling to land on the far bank, Lydia caught tantalising glimpses of the domes, arches of half a dozen or more exotic, beautiful beach houses. There was a private dock, boats, a long curve of white sand. And, behind it all, the dramatic, sharply rising background of jagged mountains, black against a sky fading to pre-dawn purple.

While she had not been fooled by the word 'cottage', had anticipated the kind of luxury that few people would ever experience, this was far beyond anything she could have imagined.

It reminded her of pictures she'd seen of the fantasy village of Portmeirion, more like a film set, or something out of a dream than anything real, and by the time the helicopter landed and she'd thanked the pilot, her heart was pounding with excitement, anticipation.

She'd been so determined to keep her reaction low-key, wanting to appear as if this was what she was used to, but that wasn't, in the end, a problem. As Kal took her hand and helped her down, she didn't have to fight to contain a *wow*. The reality was simply beyond words.

There was an open Jeep waiting for them, but she didn't rush to climb in. Instead, she walked to the edge of the landing pad so that she could look out over the creek. Eager to feel solid earth beneath her feet. To breathe in real air laden with the salty scent of the sea, wet sand, something else, sweet and heavy, that she did not recognise.

It was still quite dark, but all the way down to the beach lights threaded through huge old trees, shone in the water.

'I don't think I've ever seen anything so beautiful,' she said as Kal joined her. 'I expected sand, desert, not all this green.'

'The creek is in a valley and has a microclimate of its own,' he said. 'And Sheikh Jamal's father began an intensive tree planting programme when he took the throne fifty years ago.'

'Well, good for him.'

'Not everyone is happy. People complain that it rains more these days.'

'It rains more everywhere,' she replied, looking around for the source of the sweet, heady fragrance filling the air. 'What is that scent?' she asked.

'Jasmine.' He crossed to a shrub, broke off a piece and offered it to her with the slightest of bows. 'Welcome to Bab el Sama, Lady Rose,' he said.

# CHAPTER FIVE

LYDIA, holding the spray of tiny white flowers, didn't miss the fact that he'd put the 'Lady' back in front of her name. That his voice had taken on a more formal tone.

That was good, she told herself. Perfect, in fact.

One kiss could be overlooked, especially when it was purely medicinal, but it wouldn't do to let him think that Lady Rose encouraged such liberties.

'The luggage is loaded.'

He might as well have been done with it and added *madam*.

'The pilot won't take off until we're clear of the pad. If you are ready?'

It was right there in his tone of voice. It was the one he'd used before he'd started flirting. Before she'd started encouraging him.

She turned to look at the Jeep, where a white-robed servant was waiting to drive them to the cottage. She'd been sitting for hours and, now she was on her feet, wasn't eager to sit again unless she had to.

'Is it far?' she asked. 'I'd like to stretch my legs.'

He spoke to the driver, who answered with a shake of his head, a wave of the hand to indicate a path through the trees.

Lydia watched the exchange, then frowned.

Kal wasn't telling the man that they'd walk, she realised, but asking the way. He'd seemed so familiar with everything that she'd assumed he had been here before, but clearly this was his first time, too.

She hadn't taken much notice when he'd said his family were personae non gratae at the Ramal Hamrahn court.

*Court,* for heaven's sake. Nobody talked like that any more. But now she wondered why, for three generations, his family had lived in Europe.

What past crime was so terrible that he and his siblings had never been invited to share this idyllic summer playground with their cousins? It wasn't as if they'd be cramped for space. Even if they all turned up at the same time.

'There's a path through the gardens,' he said. Then, 'Will you be warm enough?'

'You're kidding?'

Rose had warned her that it wouldn't be hot at this time of year and maybe it wasn't for this part of the world. Compared with London in December, however, the air felt soft and balmy.

Then, as a frown creased Kal's brows, she realised that her response had been pure Lydia. Not quite on a scale with Eliza Doolittle's blooper at the races, but near enough.

She was tired and forgetting to keep up the Lady Rose act. Or maybe it was her subconscious fighting it. Wanting to say to him *Look at me, see who I really am...*

'The temperature is quite perfect,' she added. And mentally groaned. She'd be doing the whole, *How kind of you to let me come* routine if she didn't get a grip.

Didn't put some distance between them.

In a determined attempt to start as she had meant to go on— before he'd taken her hand, made her laugh—she said, 'You don't have to come with me, Kal. Just point me in the right direction and I can find my own way.'

'No doubt. However, I'd rather not have to explain to Lucy why I had to send out a search party for you.'

'Why would she ever know?'

'You're kidding?'

She ignored the wobble somewhere beneath her midriff as he repeated her words back to her as if he was mocking her, almost as if he knew. 'Actually, I'm not,' she said, knowing that it was only her guilty conscience making her think that way.

'No? Then let me explain how it would happen. At the first hint of trouble the alarm would be raised,' he explained. 'The Chief of Security would be alerted. The Emir's office would be informed, your Ambassador would be summoned—'

'Okay, okay,' she said, holding up her hands in surrender, laughing despite everything. 'I get it. If I go missing, you'll be hauled up before the Emir and asked to explain what the heck you were doing letting me wander around by myself.'

There was a momentary pause, as if he was considering the matter. Then he shrugged. 'Something like that, but all you need to worry about is the fact that Lucy would know what had happened within five minutes.'

Not something she would want to happen and, while she didn't think for one moment she'd get lost, she said, 'Point taken. Lead the way, Mr al-Zaki.'

The steps were illuminated by concealed lighting and perfectly safe, as was the path, but he took her arm, presumably in case she stumbled.

Rose wouldn't make a fuss, she told herself. No doubt someone had been holding her hand, taking her arm, keeping her safe all her life. It was what she'd wanted to escape. The constant surveillance. The cotton wool.

As he tucked her arm beneath his, she told herself that she could live with it for a week. And, as she leaned on him a little, that he would expect nothing else.

The path wound through trees and shrubs. Herbs had been planted along the edges, spilling over so that as they brushed past lavender, sage, marjoram and other, less familiar, scents filled the air.

Neither of them spoke. The only sound was the trickle of

water running, the splash of something, a fish or a frog, in a dark pool. She caught glimpses of mysterious arches, an ornate summer house, hidden among the trees. And above them the domes and towers she'd seen from the air.

'It's magical,' she said at last as, entranced, she stored up the scents, sounds, images for some day, far in the future, when she would tell her children, grandchildren about this *Arabian Nights* adventure. Always assuming she ever got to the point where she could trust a man sufficiently to get beyond arm's length flirting.

Meet someone who would look at her and see Lydia Young instead of her famous alter ego.

The thought leached the pleasure from the moment.

She'd been featured in the local newspaper when she'd first appeared as Lady Rose, had even been invited to turn up as Rose and switch on the Christmas lights one year when the local council were on a cost cutting drive and couldn't afford a real celebrity.

Even at work, wearing an unflattering uniform and with her name badge clearly visible, the customers had taken to calling her 'Rose' and she couldn't deny that she'd loved it. It had made her feel special.

Here, now, standing in her heroine's shoes, she discovered that being someone else was not enough.

That, instead of looking at Lydia and seeing Rose, she wanted someone, or maybe just Kalil al-Zaki, to look at Rose and see Lydia.

Because that was who she'd been with him.

It was Lydia who'd been afraid of taking off, whose hand he had held. Lydia he'd kissed.

But he'd never know that. And she could never tell him.

He was silent too and once she risked a glance, but the floor level lighting only threw his features into dark, unreadable shadows.

Then, as they turned a corner, the view opened up to reveal

that while behind them, above the darker bulk of the mountains, the stars still blazed, on the far side of the creek a pale edge of mauve was seeping into the pre-dawn purple.

'It's nearly dawn,' she said, surprised out of her momentary descent into self-pity. It still felt like the middle of the night, but she'd flown east, was four hours closer to the day than her mother, fast asleep in London.

She was on another continent at sunrise and, to witness it, all she had to do was stand here and wait.

Kal didn't even ask what she wanted to do. He knew.

'There's a summer house over there,' he said, urging her in the direction of another intricately decorated domed and colonnaded structure perfectly situated to enjoy the view. 'You can watch in comfort.'

'No…'

It was open at the front and there were huge cane chairs piled with cushions. Total luxury. A place to bring a book, be alone, forget everything. Maybe later. Not now.

'I don't want anything between me and the sky,' she said, walking closer to the edge of the paved terrace where the drop was guarded by a stone balustrade. 'I want to be outside where I can feel it.'

He let her go, didn't follow her and she tried not to mind.

Minding was a waste of time. Worse. It was a stupid contradiction. Distance was what she had wanted and the old lady with the wand was, it seemed, still on the job, granting wishes as if they were going out of fashion.

She should be pleased.

It wasn't as if she'd expected or needed to be diverted, amused. She had a pile of great books to amuse her, occupy her mind, and exploring the garden, wandering along the shore should be diversion enough for anyone. If the forbidden delights of Kal al-Zaki's diversionary tactics hadn't been such a potent reminder of everything she was missing. The life that she might have had if she hadn't looked like Lady Rose.

But then, as the mauve band at the edge of the sky widened, became suffused with pink, she heard a step behind her and, as she half turned, Kal settled something soft around her.

For a moment his hands lingered on her shoulders, tense and knotted from sitting for too long, and without thinking she leaned into his touch, seeking ease from his long fingers. For a moment she thought he was going to respond, but then he stepped back, putting clear air between them.

'You will get cold standing out here,' he said with a brusqueness that suggested he had, after all, been affected by their closeness. That he, too, was aware that it would be inappropriate to take it further.

'And you don't want to explain to Lucy how I caught a chill on your watch?' Light, cool, she told herself.

'That wouldn't bother me.' He joined her at the balustrade, but kept his eyes on the horizon. 'I'd simply explain that you stubbornly, wilfully insisted on standing outside in the chill of dawn, that short of carrying you inside there was nothing I could do about it. I have no doubt that she'd agree with me.'

'She would?' The idea of Rose being wilful or stubborn was so slanderous that she had to take a breath, remind herself that he was judging Rose on her behaviour, before she nodded and said, 'She would.' And vow to try a little harder—a lot harder—to be like the real thing.

'His Highness, the Emir, on the other hand,' Kal continued, 'would be certain to think that I'd personally arranged for you to go down with pneumonia in order to cause him maximum embarrassment.'

He spoke lightly enough, inviting amusement, but she didn't laugh, sensing the underlying darkness behind his words.

'Why on earth would he think that?' she asked, but more questions crowded into her head. Without waiting for him to answer, she added, 'And why do you always refer to him as His Highness or the Emir?' She made little quote marks with her fingers, something else she realised Rose would never do, and let her hands drop. 'Sheikh Jamal is your uncle, isn't he, Kal?' she prompted when he didn't answer.

'Yes,' he said shortly. Then, before she could say another word, 'Someone will bring tea in a moment.'

'This is your first visit here, too,' she said, ignoring the abrupt change of subject. 'Why is that?'

'Watch the sunrise, for heaven's sake,' he practically growled at her.

In other words, Lydia, mind your own business, she thought, unsure whether she was pleased or sorry that she'd managed to rattle him out of his good manners.

Here was a mystery. A secret.

That she wasn't the only one hiding something made her feel less guilty about the secret she was keeping for Rose, although no better about lying to him, and without another word she did as she was told.

Neither of them spoke or moved again while the darkness rolled back and the sun, still below the horizon, lit up bubbles of cloud in a blaze of colour that was reflected in the creek, the sea beyond, turning them first carmine, then pink, then liquid gold. As it grew light, the dark shapes against the water resolved themselves into traditional dhows moored amongst modern craft and beyond, sprawling over the steep bank on the far side of the creek, she could see a small town with a harbour and market which were already coming to life.

'Wow,' she said at last. 'Double wow.'

She caught a movement as Kal turned to look at her and she shrugged.

'Well, what other word is there?' she asked.

'Bab el Sama.' He said the words softly. 'The Gate of Heaven.'

She swallowed at the poetry of the name and said, 'You win.'

He shook his head and said, 'Are you done?'

'Yes. Thank you for being so patient.'

'I wouldn't have missed it,' he assured her as they turned and walked back towards the summer house—such an ordinary word for something that looked as if it had been conjured up by Aladdin's djinn—where a manservant was laying out the contents of a large tray.

The man bowed and, eyes down, said, *'Assalam alaykum, sitti. Marhaba.'*

She turned to Kal for a translation. 'He said, "Peace be upon you, Lady. Welcome."'

'What should I say in return?'

*'Shukran. Alaykum assalam,'* Kal said. 'Thank you. And upon you peace.'

The man smiled, bowed again, when she repeated it, savouring the words on her tongue, locking them away in her memory, along with Bab el Sama. He left them to enjoy their breakfast in private.

As she chose a high-backed cane chair and sank into the vivid silk cushions, Kal unwrapped a napkin nestled in a basket to reveal warm pastries.

'Hungry?'

'I seem to have done nothing but eat since I left London,' she said. 'I'll have to swim the creek once a day if I'm going to keep indulging myself this way.'

Maybe it was the thought of all that effort, but right now all she wanted to do was close her eyes and go to sleep. Tea would help, she told herself, just about managing to control a yawn.

'Is that a yes or a no?' he asked, offering her the basket.

'Breakfast *is* the most important meal of the day,' she said, succumbing to the enticing buttery smell. 'I suppose it is breakfast time?'

'It's whatever time you care to make it,' he assured her as he poured tea into two unbelievably thin china cups. 'Milk, lemon?'

'Just a touch of milk,' she said. Then, 'Should you be doing this?' He glanced at her. 'Waiting on me?'

Kal frowned, unable, for a moment, to imagine what she meant.

'Won't it ruin your image?'

'Image?'

He hadn't been brought up like his grandfather, his father, to believe he was a prince, above the mundane realities of the world. Nor, despite his Mediterranean childhood, was he one of those men who expected to live at home, waited on by a doting mother until he transferred that honour to a wife. Even if he had been so inclined, his mother had far more interesting things to do.

As had he.

His image was not about macho posturing. He had never needed to work, never would, but once he'd fallen in love with flying he had worked hard. He'd wanted to own aircraft but there was no fun in having them sit on the tarmac. He'd started Kalzak Air Services as a courier service. Now he flew freight worldwide. And he employed men and women—hundreds of them—on their qualifications and personal qualities first, last and everything in between.

'Hanif nursed his first wife, nursed Lucy, too, when she was injured,' he said.

'He did?'

'Lucy has not told you?'

'Only that he loved her.'

'He loved his first wife, too.' The girl who had been chosen for him. A traditional arranged marriage. 'He has been twice blessed.'

'Maybe he is a man who knows how to love,' she said.

Was that the answer?

It was not a concept he was comfortable with and, remembering what Lucy had said about Rose not being able to lift a finger without someone taking a photograph of her, he carried his own cup towards the edge of the promontory and leaned against the parapet. A man enjoying the view. It was what anyone would do in such a place.

The sun was in the wrong direction to reflect off a lens that would betray a paparazzo lying in wait to snatch a photograph. Not that he imagined they would ever be that careless. The only obvious activity was on the dhows as their crews prepared to head out to sea for a day's fishing.

As he scanned the wider panorama, the distant shore, he saw only a peaceful, contented community waking to a new day, going about its business. He let the scene sink into his bones the way parched earth sucked up rain.

As a boy, his grandfather would have stood in this same spot, looking at the creek, the town, the desert beyond it, certain in the knowledge that every drop of water, every grain of sand would, *insh'Allah,* one day be his.

Except that Allah had not willed it. His grandfather had followed his heart instead of his head and, as a result, had been judged unworthy. A lesson he had learned well.

He drained his cup, took one last look, then returned to the summer house.

Sparrows, pecking at a piece of pastry, flew up at his approach and a single look was enough to tell him that Rose had fallen asleep, tea untouched, croissant untasted.

And, now that the sun had risen high enough to banish the shadows from the summer house and illuminate her clear, fair skin, he could see the faint violet smudges beneath her eyes.

Clearly sleep had eluded her aboard the plane and a long day, a long flight, had finally caught up with her. This was no light doze and he did not attempt to wake her, but as he bent and caught her beneath the knees she sighed.

'Shh,' he said, easing her arm over his shoulder, around his neck. 'Hold on.'

On some level of consciousness she must have heard him because, as he lifted her out of the chair, she curled her hand around his neck and tucked her head into the hollow of his shoulder.

She wasn't anywhere near as light, as ethereal as she looked, he discovered as he carried her along the path to Lucy and Han's seaside retreat. Not an angel, but a real, solid woman and he was glad that the huge doors stood wide to welcome her.

He walked straight in, picking up a little group of women who, clucking anxiously, rushed ahead to open doors, circled round them tutting with disapproval and finally stood in his way when he reached her bedroom.

'Move,' he said, 'or I'll drop her.'

They scattered with little squeals of outrage, then, as he laid her on the bed, clicked his fingers for a cover in a manner that would have made his grandfather proud—and he would have protested was utterly alien to him—they rushed to do his bidding.

He removed her shoes but, about to reach for the button at her waist to make her more comfortable, he became aware of a silence, a collectively held breath.

He turned to look at the women clustered behind him, their shocked faces. And, remembering himself, took a step back.

That he could have undressed her in a completely detached manner had the occasion demanded it was not in question. But this was not London, or New York, or Paris. This was a world where a man did not undress a woman unless he was married to her. He should not even be in her room.

'Make her comfortable,' he said with a gesture that would have done his grandfather proud. Maybe it was the place calling to his genes, he thought as he closed the door behind him, leaving the women to their task.

Then, to an old woman who'd settled herself, cross-legged, in front of the door like a palace guard, 'When she wakes she should have a massage.'

'It will be done, sidi.'

Lord…

'Don't call me that,' he said, straightening, easing his own aching limbs.

'You don't want to be given your title, Sheikh?' she asked, clearly not in the slightest bit in awe of him. 'Your grandfather wanted to be the Emir.'

About to walk away, he stopped, turned slowly back to face her.

'You knew him?'

'When he was a boy. A young man. Before he was foolish.'

She was the first person he'd met in Ramal Hamrah who was prepared to admit that. He sat before her, crossing his legs so that the soles of his feet were tucked out of sight.

'Here? You knew him here?'

'Here. In Rumaillah. At Umm al Sama. He was the wild one. Headstrong.' She shook her head. 'And he was stubborn, like his father. Once he'd said a thing, that was it.' She brushed her palms together in a gesture he'd seen many times. It signalled an end to discussion. That the subject was closed. 'They were two rocks.' She tilted her head in a birdlike gesture, examining him closely. 'You look like him,' she said after a while. 'Apart from the beard. A man should have a beard.'

He rubbed his hand self-consciously over his bare chin. He had grown a beard, aware that to be clean-shaven was the western way; it would be something else the Emir could hold against him.

'My grandfather doesn't have a beard these days,' he told her. The chemo baldness hadn't bothered him nearly as much as the loss of this symbol of his manhood and Kal had taken a razor to his own beard in an act of solidarity. It had felt odd for a while, but he'd got used to it.

'They say that he is dying,' she said. He did not ask who had said. Gossip flowed through the harem like water down the Nile.

'But still stubborn,' he replied. 'He refuses to die anywhere but in the place he still calls home.'

She nodded, 'You are stubborn, too,' she said, reaching up to pat his hand. 'You will bring him home, *insh'Allah*. It is your destiny.'

'Who are you?' he asked, with a sudden sinking feeling, the certainty that he had just made a complete fool of himself.

'I am Dena. I was found, out there,' she said with the wave of an elegant hand, the rattle of gold on her skinny wrists. 'Your great-grandmother took me into her house. Made me her daughter.'

Oh, terrific. This woman was the adopted child of the Khatib and he'd spoken to her as if she were a servant. But from the way she'd settled herself in front of Rose's bedroom door…

He'd been brought up on his grandfather's stories, had studied his family, this country, clung to a language that his father had all but forgotten, but he still had so much to learn.

He uncurled himself, got to his feet. 'My apologies, *sitti*,' he said with a formal bow.

'You have his charm, too,' she said. 'When you speak to him tell him that his sister Dena remembers him with fondness.' Then, 'Go.' She waved him away. 'Go. I will watch over your lady while you sleep.'

His lady…

Dena's words echoed in his mind as he stood beneath the shower, igniting again the memory of Rose's lips, warm, vital as they'd softened beneath him, parted for him. His mouth burned but as he sucked his lower lip into his mouth, ran a tongue over it, he tasted Rose and, instead of cooling it down, the heat surged like a contagion through his body.

*Do you want me to protect her or make love to her…?*

Lucy had not answered his question, but it would have made no difference either way. He was not free. He flipped the shower to cold and, lifting his face to the water, stood beneath it until he was chilled to the bone.

And still he burned.

# CHAPTER SIX

LYDIA woke in slow gentle ripples of consciousness. Blissful comfort was the first stage. The pleasure of smooth, sweet-smelling sheets, the perfect pillow and, unwilling to surrender the pleasure, she turned over and fell back into its embrace.

The jewelled light filtering through ornate wooden shutters, colours dancing on white walls, seeping through her eyelids, came next.

She opened her eyes and saw an ornate band of tiny blue and green tiles shimmering like the early morning creek. She turned onto her back, looked up at a high raftered cedar wood ceiling.

It was true then. Not a dream.

'Bab el Sama.' She said the name out loud, savouring the feel of it in her mouth. The Gate of Heaven. '*Marhaba...*' Welcome. 'Kalil al-Zaki...' Trouble.

'You are awake, *sitti?*'

What?

She sat up abruptly. There was a woman, her head, body swathed in an enfolding black garment, sitting cross-legged in front of a pair of tall carved doors, as if guarding the entrance.

She rose with extraordinary grace and bowed her head. 'I am Dena, *sitti*. Princess Lucy called me, asked me to take care of you.'

'She seems to have called everyone,' Lydia said.

So much for being alone!

She threw off the covers, then immediately grabbed them back, clutching them to her chest, as she realised that she was naked.

Realised that she had no memory of getting that way. Only of the sunrise with Kal, soft cushions, the scent of buttery pastry. Of closing her eyes.

'Bin Zaki carried you here, *sitti*. We made you comfortable.'

Lydia swallowed, not quite sure how she felt about that. Whether it was worse that an unknown 'we' had undressed her sleeping body or Kal.

The woman, Dena, picked up a robe, held it out so that she could turn and slip her arms through the sleeves, wrap it around her, preserve a little of her modesty before sliding out of the bed.

It clung to her, soft and light as the touch of a butterfly wing, leaving her feeling almost as exposed as if she was wearing nothing at all. The kind of thing a pampered concubine might have worn. With a sudden quickening of something almost like fear, laced through with excitement, she said, 'Where is Kal?'

'He went to the stables.' The woman's eyes, as she handed her the glass of juice she'd poured from a flask, saw the flush that heated her skin and smiled knowingly. 'He took a horse,' she said. Then, 'I will bathe you and then you will have a massage.'

What?

'That won't be necessary,' she said.

'Bin Zaki ordered it so. Princess Lucy always needs a massage when she comes home.'

'Really?'

But the woman had opened a door that led into a bathroom that was out of a fantasy. A deep sunken tub. A huge shower with side jets. A seat big enough for two.

'Which?' Dena asked.

'The shower,' Lydia said, dismissing the disturbing image of sinking into the huge tub, sharing it with Kal.

She really, really needed something to clear her head, wake her up.

Dena turned it on, adjusted the temperature, apparently oblivious of the fact that her floor length black dress was getting wet. Apparently waiting for her to shed the robe and step into the shower so that she could wash her.

No, no, no...

Lydia swallowed, said, 'I can manage. Really.'

She nodded. 'Come into the next room when you are ready and I will ease the ache in your shoulder.'

Lydia stared after her. Raised her left hand to her right shoulder, the one that ached when it was cold or damp. After a long shift on the checkout. The legacy of years of lifting other people's groceries across a scanner.

How did she know? What had given her away?

She shook her head.

Nothing. Dena couldn't know that she was a fake. If she did, the whole house of cards would be tumbling around her ears by now, she told herself as she slipped out of the wrap, stepped under the warm water.

If she was a trained masseuse she would be observant, that was all, would notice the slightest imbalance. It didn't mean anything.

She might have slept awkwardly on the plane or strained it in a hundred ways.

She turned up the heat and let the water pound her body, easing an ache which, until that moment, she'd been scarcely aware of herself.

Lathered herself in rich soap.

Washed her hair.

Putting off, for as long as possible, the moment when, wrapped in a towel that covered her from breast to ankle, her hair wrapped in a smaller one, she would have to submit herself to the ministrations of the slightly scary Dena.

But as she lay down and Dena's hands found the knots in her muscles, soothed away the tension of the last twenty-four hours, all the stress floated away and she surrendered to total pampering.

Wrapped tenderly in a robe, seated in a chair that tilted back, her hair was released and unseen hands massaged her scalp, gently combed out her hair, while a young girl did miraculous things to her feet, her hands.

Painted her nails, drew patterns with henna.

By the time they were finished, she was so utterly relaxed that when one of the girls held out a pair of exquisite French knickers she stepped into them without a flicker of embarrassment.

Slipped into a matching lace bra and left it for someone else to fasten.

Held up her arms as Dena slipped a loose silk kaftan over her head that had certainly not been part of the wardrobe packed by Rose.

It floated over her, a mist of blue, then settled over her shoulders, her arms, falling to the floor before nimble fingers fastened the dozen or more silk-covered buttons that held it together at her breast.

Then she stepped into a pair of soft thong sandals that were placed in front of her.

A week of this and she'd be ruined for real life, she thought, pulling her lips back against her teeth so that she wouldn't grin out loud.

Wow! Wow! Wow!

Thank you, Rose! I hope you're enjoying every second of your freedom. Having the most wonderful time.

And, with that thought, reality rushed back as she looked around for the clutch bag she'd been carrying.

A word and it was in her hand and she took out her mobile phone to send the agreed 'arrived safely' message, followed by another more detailed message to her mother. Not just to let her know that she'd got to her destination without mishap, but that the apartment was great and she was having a great time.

So far, so true. Unless... Did kissing Kal count as a mishap?

She looked at the message doubtfully, then, with a rueful smile, hit 'send', grateful that her mother had insisted that overseas mobile calls were too expensive, that the occasional text was all she expected. She would never be able to bluff her way through an entire week of this, not with her mother. With Kal…

She looked up and realised that everyone was waiting to hear what she wanted to do next.

She slipped the phone into a pocket in the seam of the kaftan and said, 'May I look around?'

Dena led the way, down a series of steps to a lower level entrance lobby with a two-storey domed ceiling richly decorated in floral designs with tiny ceramic tiles, her helpers following, all anxious to see her reaction. Clearly wanting her to love this place they called home.

They waited patiently while she stopped, turned slowly, looking up in awe at the workmanship.

'This is a holiday cottage?' she asked in amazement. 'It's so beautiful!'

Dena was unreadable, but the two younger women were clearly delighted.

The tour took in a formal dining room where ornate carved doors had been folded back to reveal a terrace and, below it, set in a private walled garden, a swimming pool.

More steps and then Dena said, 'This is the room the family use when they are here.'

Furnished with richly coloured sofas and jewel-bright oriental rugs that softened the polished wooden floor, Lydia might have been totally overwhelmed by its sheer size, but then she spotted a fluffy yellow toy duck half hidden amongst the cushions.

It was a reminder that this was someone's holiday home, a place where children ran and played. She picked it up and held it for a moment and when she looked up she saw that Dena was smiling.

'It is Jamal's,' she said. 'He left it there to keep his place while he was away.'

'Bless,' she said, carefully tucking it back where she'd found it and, looking around, saw the touches that made this unbelievably grand room a home.

The box filled with toys. A pile of books that suggested Lucy's favourite holiday activity was reading. A child's drawing of the creek, framed as lovingly as an old master. Children's books in English and Arabic.

'You like children?' Dena asked as she picked up an alphabet colouring book similar to one she'd had as a child. Except that the alphabet was Arabic.

She nodded. 'Even the little monsters...'

Even the little monsters who whined and nagged their stressed mothers for sweets at the checkout. Their soft little mouths, big eyes that could be coaxed so quickly from tears to a smile with a little attention.

She was so relaxed that she'd completely forgotten to guard her tongue but, while Dena regarded her thoughtfully, the younger women giggled, repeating 'little monsters' as if they knew only too well what she meant.

She managed a shrug and Dena, making no comment, folded back doors similar to the ones in the dining room, opening up one side of the room to the garden so that Lydia could step out onto a wide terrace that overlooked the creek.

'All children love Bab el Sama,' she said. 'You will bring your children here.'

It sounded more like a statement than a question and Lydia swallowed.

She had two careers and no time for romance, even if she could ever trust a man again sufficiently to let him get that close.

Maybe Kal was the answer. He, at least, wouldn't be pretending...

She, on the other hand, would be.

Since the one thing she demanded of a man was total honesty, to kiss with a lie on her lips was not something she could live with, no matter how alluring the temptation.

'I'm sure they have a wonderful time,' she said, responding to her first comment, ignoring the second as she walked quickly to the edge of the terrace as if to take a closer look at the beach.

They were much lower here than on the bluff where she'd watched the sunrise, not more than twenty feet above the beach. And, looking around, she thought that the adults must love it too.

There were pots overflowing with geraniums, still flowering in December, the rustle and clack of palm fronds in the light breeze, a snatch of unfamiliar music carrying across the glittering water.

It was peaceful, beautiful, with a delicious warmth that seeped into the bones and invited her to lift her face to the sun and smile as if she were a sunflower.

Even as she did that, a movement caught her eye and below, on the beach, she saw a horseman galloping along the edge of the surf, robes streaming out behind him.

The horse, its hooves a blur in the spray, seemed to be almost flying, elemental, a force of nature. Lydia's breath caught in her throat and she took a step closer, her hand lifting towards him as if reaching to catch hold, be lifted up to fly with him.

'It is Bin Zaki,' Dena said, but Lydia knew that.

He might have shed his designer suit, donned a robe, hidden his dark curls beneath a *keffiyeh,* but his chiselled face, the fierce hawkish nose were imprinted on her memory and, as he flashed by in a swirl of cloth, hooves, spray, the profile was unmistakable.

'He is chasing his demons. So like his grandfather.'

For a moment she didn't respond, scarcely registered what the woman had said, but Kal had gone, lost from sight as the beach curved around massive rocks, the final fling of the mountain range behind them. And already the sea was smoothing away the hoof prints, rubbing out all trace of his passing.

She turned to discover that Dena was watching her and, suddenly coming back to reality, she dropped her hand self-consciously.

'Demons? What demons?'

'He will tell you in his own good time. Do you need anything, *sitti?*'

Only to be held, enfolded, caressed, but not by some anonymous, faceless figure. All the longings and desires that haunted her had become focused on one man and she turned back to the empty beach as if his spirit was still there for her to reach out and touch.

'I think I'll take a walk,' she said, suddenly self-conscious, certain that Dena knew exactly what she was thinking. 'Explore a little. Is there anywhere I shouldn't go?'

'Bab el Sama is yours, *sitti.*'

Dena left her alone to explore and she skirted the terrace, noticing how cleverly it was shielded from the creek by the trees so that no one from below would be able to see the royal family at play.

Taking a path, she found steps that led invitingly downwards in the direction of the beach but, conscious of the silk kaftan flowing around her ankles, she turned instead along a path that led upward through the garden.

After the crash that had killed her father and left her mother in a wheelchair, she and her mother had moved from their small house with a garden into a ground floor flat that had been adapted for a wheelchair user.

She'd missed the garden but, ten years old, she'd understood the necessity and knew better than to say anything that would hurt her mother. It was the hand that life had dealt but even then she'd used her pocket money to buy flowering pot plants from the market. Had grown herbs on the windowsill.

This garden was like a dream. Little streams ran down through the trees, fell over rocks to feed pools where carp rose at her appearance.

There were exquisite summer houses tucked away. Some were for children, with garden toys. Some, with comfortable chairs, were placed to catch a stunning view.

One, with a copper roof turned green with verdigris, was laid
with rich carpets on which cushions had been piled, and looked
like a lovers' hideaway. She could imagine lying there with Kal,
his lips pressed against her throat as he unfastened the buttons...

She lifted her hand to her breast, shook her head, trying to
rid herself of an image that was so powerful that she could feel
his hands, his mouth on her body.

As she backed away there was a scuffle near her feet as a
lizard disappeared in a flurry of emerald tail. For a moment she
stared at the spot, not sure whether she'd imagined it. Then she
looked up and saw Kal standing just a few feet away.

The *keffiyeh* had fallen from his head and lay gathered about
his neck. His robes were made of some loosely woven cream
material and the hem was heavy with sea water and sand. As
they stood there, silent, still, a trickle of sweat ran from his
temple into the dust on his cheek.

After what seemed like an age he finally moved, lifting his
elbow to wipe his face on his sleeve.

'I've been riding,' he said wearily.

'I saw you. You looked as if you were flying,' she said.

'That's me,' he said, the corner of his mouth lifting in a self-
mocking smile. 'Addicted to the air.' He took a step forward
but Lydia, almost dizzy with the scent of leather, of the sea
clinging to his clothes, of tangy fresh sweat that her body was
responding to like an aphrodisiac, didn't move.

Hot, sweaty he exuded a raw sexual potency and she wanted
to touch his face. Kiss the space between his thumb and palm,
taste the leather; lean into him and bury her face in his robes,
breathe him in. Wanted to feel those long, powerful hands that
had so easily controlled half a ton of muscle and bone in full
flight, on her own body.

She cooled her burning lip with the tip of her tongue, then,
realising how that must look, said, 'Maybe my problem with
flying is that I didn't start in the right place.'

He frowned. 'You don't ride?'

'No.' Having studied every aspect of her alter ego's life, she knew that while most little girls of her class would have been confidently astride her first pony by the time she was three, Rose was not one of them. 'But, if I had to choose, I think I'd prefer it to fishing.'

His smile was a lazy thing that began in the depths of his eyes, barely noticeable if you weren't locked in to every tiny response. No more than a tiny spark that might so easily have been mistaken for a shaft of sunlight finding a space between the leaves to warm the darkness. Then the creases that fanned out around them deepened a little, the skin over his cheekbones tightened and lifted. Only then did his mouth join in with a slightly lopsided *gotcha* grin.

'Here's the deal,' he said. 'You let me take you fishing and I'll teach you to ride.'

His voice, his words seemed to caress her so that it sounded more like a sexual proposition than a simple choice between this or that outdoor activity. Standing there in the dappled sunlight, every nerve-ending at attention, sensitized by desire, she knew that if he reached out, touched her, she would buckle, dissolve and if he carried her into the summer house and laid her amongst the cushions, nothing could save her.

That she wouldn't want to be saved.

This powerful, instant attraction had nothing to do with who they were. Or weren't. It was pure chemistry. Names, titles meant nothing.

She lowered her lids, scarcely able to breathe. 'Is that your final offer?'

His voice soft, dangerously seductive, he said, 'How about if I offered to bait your hook for you?'

Baited, hooked, landed...

She swallowed, cooled her burning lower lip with her tongue. 'How could I resist such an inducement?'

A step brought him alongside her and he took her chin in

his hand, ran the pad of his thumb over her mouth in an exploratory sweep as if to test its heat.

'It is a date, Rose.'

He was so close that she could see the grains of sand thrown up by the flying hooves which clung to his face and, as she closed her eyes to breathe in the pure essence of the man, his mouth touched hers, his tongue lightly tracing her lower lip, imitating the route her own had taken seconds before, as if tasting her.

Before she could react, clutch at him to stop herself from collapsing at his feet, it was over.

'You will fish with me this afternoon. I will ride with you at dawn.'

'Perfect,' she managed through a throat that felt as if it was stuffed with cotton wool. Through lips that felt twice their normal size.

Then, as she opened her eyes, he stepped back and said, 'You might want to wear something a little less...distracting.'

Before she could respond, he strode away in a swirl of robes and she did not move until she was quite alone.

Only when the path was quite empty, the only sound—apart from the pounding of her heart—was the rattle of palm fronds high above her, did she finally look down, see for herself how the light breeze was moulding the thin blue silk to her body so that it outlined every contour. Her thighs, the gentle curve of her belly. The hard, betraying, touch-me peaks of her breasts.

# CHAPTER SEVEN

KAL stood beneath the pounding icy shower. He did not need hot water; the heat coming off him was turning the water to steam.

He closed his eyes but it didn't help. Without visual distraction, the image of Rose Napier, silk clinging to every curve, filled his head, obliterating everything from his mind but her.

If he had ever doubted her innocence, he was now utterly convinced of it. No woman who had a scintilla of experience would have let a man see such naked desire shining out of her eyes, been so unconscious of the *come-and-take-me* signals her body was semaphoring in response to his nearness. Given him such power over her.

But maybe they were both out of their depth.

Preoccupied with his own concerns and apparently immune to this pale beauty that the entire world appeared to be in love with, his guard had been down.

Knocked sideways from his first sight of her and, knowing that he wouldn't sleep, he'd gone to the stables, determined to blow away the demands of his body in hard physical activity.

But as hard as he'd ridden he could not shake loose the image of those blue eyes. One moment *keep-your-distance* cool, the next sparkling with life, excitement. A touch of mischief.

Almost, he thought, as if she were two women.

The adored, empathetic public figure—as flawless and beautiful as a Bernini marble, as out of reach as the stars.

And this private, flesh and blood woman whose eyes appealed for his touch, for him to take her, bring her to life.

Living with those eyes, those seductive lips that drew him to her, would not make for a comfortable week. And he'd just made it a thousand times worse.

He'd ridden off the sexual energy that had built over their long flight. Had been totally in control, with the self-discipline to keep his hands off her.

All he'd had to do was keep his distance, leave it to her to initiate any outings. He had his own agenda and it certainly didn't include getting involved with a woman, especially one who was a national icon.

Until he'd taken a turn in the path and saw her standing before him, her hair hanging like silk around her shoulders. Wearing an embroidered silk kaftan that exactly matched eyes shining like a woman on her wedding night.

And he'd been the one insisting that the two of them should spend time alone together on a boat.

Offering to teach her to ride.

Unable to resist touching her lip with his thumb, his tongue, wanting to test the heat, knowing that it was for him.

It had taken every ounce of self-discipline to stop himself from carrying her into the pavilion hidden in the trees behind her. Making her his.

To force himself to step back, walk away.

He flipped off the water, stepped from the shower, grabbed a towel and wrapped it round him.

His clothes had been pressed and hung up but someone, Dena, probably, had added an array of casual and formal robes for his use while he was at Bab el Sama.

The kind of clothes that Hanif would wear. A sheikh, relaxing in the privacy of his own home, with his children around him.

It was Dena, undoubtedly, who'd dressed Rose in that silk dress, had painted her hands with henna. He frowned, wondering what she thought she was doing.

He shook his head. Rose was on holiday in an exotic location and no doubt Lucy had ordered that her friend be totally pampered.

She certainly looked a great deal more rested. Unlike him. He lifted his shoulders, easing them, then reached for his cellphone and called his grandfather at the clinic.

After he'd asked how he was, as if he didn't know—in desperate pain but stubbornly refusing palliative care until he was permitted to return home to die—and getting the same answer, he said, 'I met someone today who knew you.'

'And is prepared to admit it?'

'She said that you were stubborn, *Jaddi*. But charming—'

There was a short harsh laugh, then, 'She?'

'She said, "Tell him that his sister Dena remembers him with fondness."'

'Dena?' There was a rare catch in the old man's voice. 'She is well?'

'She is well,' he confirmed. 'She said it was time you were home.'

'Tell her... Tell her I will be there, *insh'Allah*. Tell her that I will not die until I have kissed her.'

'It will be so, *Jaddi'l habeeb*,' Kal said softly. 'I swear it.'

He put down the phone, spent a moment reminding himself why he was here, gathering himself.

Then he pulled out the jeans he'd brought with him, chose a loose long-sleeved white shirt from the wardrobe and pulled it over his head and stepped into thong sandals that seemed more suitable than any of the shoes he'd brought with him.

As he picked up the phone to stow it in his pocket, it rang. Caller ID warned him that it was Lucy and he said, 'Checking up on me, Princess?'

She laughed. 'Why? What are you up to?' Then, not waiting for an answer, 'I just wanted to be sure that Rose arrived safely.'

'So why not call her?'

'She wants to cut herself off from everyone while she's

away. She wants to think about the future without anyone else offering their opinions, clouding the picture.'

'Instead, she got me,' he said. 'Tell me, was there a single word of truth in what you told me?'

'Absolutely. Cross my heart,' she swore. 'Why do you think her grandfather was so desperate to stop her? He doesn't want her doing anything as dangerous as thinking for herself, not without someone on hand to guide her thoughts in the right direction.'

'And that would be in the direction of the marriage he's arranged?' he asked casually enough, despite the fact that the thought of another man touching her sent a shaft of possessive heat driving deep into his groin.

'She's longing for a family, children of her own, Kal, and I think she's very nearly desperate enough to marry Rupert Devenish to get them.'

'What other reason is there for a woman to marry?' he asked.

Or a man, for that matter.

Far better to have people who had known you all your life, who understood your strengths and weaknesses, to seek a bride whose temperament, expectations matched your own, than rely on unbridled passion that, no matter how intense the heat, would soon become ashes. He'd seen it happen. His grandfather, his father…

'Oh, pish-posh,' Lucy said with the impatience of a woman who'd found a rare love and thought he should be making an effort to do the same. 'How is she?'

'Rose? She slept for a while, but now she's exploring the garden.'

'On her own?'

'I have no doubt that your Dena has someone within call.' Someone who would have seen him kissing her? 'She's safe enough,' he said abruptly. 'And we're about to have lunch.'

'Maybe when you've eaten you'll be in a better mood. Perhaps I should call you then?'

'No. Really. I've just spoken to my grandfather. And, as for your Rose, well, she isn't quite what I expected. I imagined un-ruffled serenity.'

'Oh? In what way is she not serene?'

In the quick blush that warmed her pale skin, in her eyes, a mouth, a body that gave away too much.

'Well,' he said, pushing away the disturbing images, 'I would have welcomed a warning that she's a nervous flyer.'

'Rose? I never knew that. How did she cope with the heli-copter?' Her concern was genuine enough, Kal decided, giving her the benefit of the doubt.

'I managed to keep her distracted.' Before she could ask him how, he added, 'I was surprised to discover that she doesn't ride.'

'I think a pony bolted with her when she was little.' He could see the tiny frown as she tried to remember. 'Something like that.'

'Well, she appears to be willing to give it another go.'

'You're going to take her riding?'

'Amuse and entertain her, that was the brief.'

'Absolutely. I'm glad you're taking it so seriously. But the reason for my call is to give you advance warning that Rose should be getting a courtesy visit from Princess Sabirah later in the week. The household will be warned of her arrival, but I thought you might welcome a little extra time to prepare yourself.'

'Thank you, Lucy. If I haven't sufficiently expressed my grat—'

'It's little enough in return for everything you've done for my charity, Kal. Just do me one favour. Don't tell Rose that I was checking up on her.'

'I won't. Lucy…'

He hesitated. He knew his doubts were foolish. Lady Rose Napier had been hand delivered to him by her security guard…

'Yes?' she prompted.

'Nothing. Take care.'

He disconnected, pushed the phone into his back pocket and, bearing in mind that it was his duty to keep her safe, he went to find Rose.

Lydia resisted the urge to fling herself into the nearest pool to cool herself down. Instead, she walked the winding paths, swiftly at first, outrunning feelings she could not control, until her breath was coming in short gasps and she almost collapsed into a seat that seemed to have been placed precisely for that purpose.

She sat there for an age while her breathing returned to normal and the heat gradually faded from her skin, attempting to make sense of what had happened.

She might as well try to catch mist in her hand.

There *was* no sense in it. Love—or just plain lust—as she knew to her cost, made fools of everyone.

'Get a grip, Lydie,' she said intently, startling a bird from the tree above her. 'Rose is depending on you. This madness will go away.' Then, after a long time, 'It will go away.'

By the time she returned to the terrace her flush might easily have been put down to nothing more than a brisk walk on a sunny day.

Just as well, because one of the girls who'd taken care of her was sitting cross-legged in the shade, embroidering a piece of silk.

'You will eat, *sitti?*' she asked, rising gracefully to her feet.

Food was the last thing on her mind, but it had been a long time since the croissant that she'd barely tasted and eating was a proven distraction for heartache.

'Thank you... I'm sorry, I don't know your name.'

'It is Yatimah, *sitti.*'

'Yatimah,' she repeated, rolling the word around her mouth, tasting the strangeness of it. 'Thank you, Yatimah. Your English is very good.'

'Princess Lucy has taught me. She speaks Arabic as if she

was born here, but her mother comes sometimes. From New Zealand. And her friends from England.'

'And they do not,' Lydia said.

'A few words,' she said with a smile.

'Will you teach me?'

'*Nam,*' she said. And giggled. 'That means yes.'

'*Nam,*' she repeated. Then, remembering the word Kal had taught her, she said, '*Shukran.* Thank you.' And received a delighted clap. Encouraged, she asked, 'What is "good morning"?'

'Good morning is *sabah alkhair* and the reply is *sabah alnur.*'

Lydia tried it and got the response from Yatimah who, an eager teacher, then said, 'Good afternoon is *masa alkhair* and the reply *masa alnur.* And goodnight is—'

'*Leila sa'eeda.*'

Startled by Kal's voice from the doorway, Yatimah scuttled away, leaving Lydia alone with him.

The last time he'd kissed her, she'd managed to dismiss it as if it was nothing. They both knew that wasn't going to happen this time and for a moment neither of them moved, spoke.

'Lucy called,' he said at last, stepping onto the terrace.

He'd showered and changed into a loose white collarless shirt that hung to his hips. Soft faded jeans. Strong, bare feet pushed into thong sandals. The clothes were unremarkable but with that thin high-bridged nose, polished olive skin, dark hair curling onto his neck, he looked very different from the man in the suit who'd met her at the airport. More like some desert lord surveying his world.

'She wanted to be sure you'd arrived safely.'

'Then why didn't she call me?' Lydia asked, brave in the knowledge that if she'd rung Rose, by the magic of the cellphone, she'd have got Rose, wherever she was. Except, of course, that Rose didn't know anything about Kal. She'd need to send a message, she thought, her hand going to the phone in her pocket, warn her…

'My own reaction,' he replied, 'but she seemed to be under

the impression that you'd rather not talk to anyone from home. That you did not want to be disturbed.'

...or maybe not.

He turned to her in expectation of polite denial.

Being a lookalike was an acting role, stepping into the shoes of another person, copying the moves, the gestures, the facial expressions. Practising the voice until it became her own. But nothing that Rose had ever done had prepared her for this.

In a situation like this, all she had to fall back on was the supermarket checkout girl with the fast mouth.

And that girl wouldn't let him off with a polite anything. That girl would look him in the eye, lift an eyebrow and say, 'She should have thought about that before she invited you to my party.'

Just like that.

If she'd hoped to raise a smile, she would have been sadly disappointed.

Apart from the slightest contraction of a muscle at the corner of his mouth—as if she needed any encouragement to look at it—his expression didn't alter for so long that, but for that tiny giveaway, she might have wondered if he'd actually heard her.

Then, with the merest movement of his head, he acknowledged the hit and said, 'No doubt that's why she asked me not to tell you she'd called.'

'So why did you?' she demanded, refusing to back down, play the lady. She might not know what Rose would do under these circumstances, but she jolly well knew what she should do after that very close encounter in the garden.

That had gone far beyond simple flirting. Far beyond what had happened in the helicopter, where his kiss had been simple enough. It had been her own reaction that had turned into something much more complex; fear, strangeness, the need to cling to something safe would do that and it was easy enough to dismiss as an aberration.

But what had happened in the garden was different.

He'd touched her mouth as if marking her as his, taken her lower lip into his mouth as intimately as a lover, certain of his welcome.

And she had welcomed him.

That moment had been an acknowledgement of the intense attraction that had been bubbling beneath the surface from the moment she had walked into the airport and found him waiting for her.

It was a dance where they circled one another, getting closer and closer. Touching briefly. Moving apart as they fought it but, like two moths being drawn closer and closer to a candle, totally unable to resist the fatal attraction, even though they both knew they would go down in flames.

Except that she had no choice. She had to withstand the temptation or tell him the truth, because she knew how it felt to be made love to by someone who was acting. Knew how betrayed she'd felt.

And she couldn't tell him the truth. Couldn't betray Rose for her own selfish desires. Not that he'd want her if she did. He was not a man to accept a fake. A copy. If he knew the truth he'd lose interest, turn away.

And if he didn't...

'Kal...'

'You are hungry?'

Her life seemed to be happening in slow motion, Lydia thought. Neither of them moved or made a move to answer Dena's query for what seemed like forever.

It did not matter. Apparently oblivious to the tension between them, she bustled across the terrace to a table set beneath the trees, issuing orders to the staff that trailed after her.

A cloth was laid, food was set out.

'Come, eat,' she said, waving them towards the table.

Kal moved first, held out a chair for her, and she managed to unstick her feet from the flagstones and join him at the table.

'This looks wonderful, Dena,' she said, trying very hard to ignore his hands grasping the back of her chair, the beautiful bones of his wrists, the dark hair exposed where he'd folded back the sleeves of his shirt, the woody scent of soap and shampoo as she sat down and he bent over her to ease the chair forward.

It was like living inside a kaleidoscope of the senses. Everything was heightened. The food glowed, gleamed with colour, enticed with spices. The arm of her chair, worn smooth by many hands. The starchy smell, the feel of the damask cloth against her legs. A silence so intense that she could almost feel it.

Then a bird fluttered down, anticipating crumbs, and gradually everything began to move again and she realised that Dena was speaking. That both she and Kal were looking at her.

'What?' she asked.

Dena excused herself, leaving Kal to pass on the message, but he shook his head as if it was nothing important and instead took her on a culinary tour of the table.

Rice cooked with saffron and studded with pine nuts and sultanas. Locally caught fish. Chicken. Jewelled salads. Small cheeses made from goats' milk.

'It's a feast,' she said with every appearance of pleasure, even though alarm bells were going off in her head, certain that she'd missed something. That somehow they knew... 'I just hope Dena does not expect me to eat it all. I usually have a sandwich for lunch.'

'And here I was thinking that you spent every day at a lavish lunch, raising money for charity.'

His words were accompanied by a wry smile and the bells quietened a little, the tension seeping away beneath the honeyed warmth of his voice, his eyes.

'Not more than once a week,' she assured him. Then, managing a smile of her own, 'Maybe twice. But I only taste the food.'

'A taste will satisfy Dena. None of the food will be wasted.' He took her plate. 'Rice?'

'A spoonful,' she replied, repeating the same word each

time he offered her a new dish. He put no more than a morsel of each on her plate but, by the time he had finished, it was still an awful lot of food to eat in the middle of the day and she regarded it doubtfully.

'It will be a long time until dinner, Rose. We eat late. And you're going to need plenty of energy before then.' She looked up. 'We're going fishing, remember?'

'Is it hard work? I thought you just sat with a rod and waited for the fish to bite.' She picked up a fork. 'Was that what you were arranging with Dena?'

He hesitated for a moment, as if he had some unpleasant news to impart, and the bells began jangling again.

'Kal?'

He shook his head. 'It was nothing to do with this afternoon. She's had a message from Rumaillah. It seems that the Emir's wife has decided to pay you a courtesy call.'

The fork in Lydia's hand shook and the waiting sparrows dived on the scattered grains of rice.

'The Emir's wife?'

'I know that you hoped to be totally private here, Rose, but I'm sure you understand that Princess Sabirah could not ignore your presence in her country.'

Lydia felt the colour drain from her face.

When Rose had asked her to do this it had all seemed so simple. Once she was out of the country there would be nothing to do but indulge herself in one of those perfectly selfish holidays that everyone dreamed about occasionally. The kind where you could read all day and all night if you wanted to. Swim. Take a walk on the beach. Do what you wanted without having to think about another person.

And, like Rose, do some serious thinking about the future.

She'd had ten good years as Rose's lookalike and had no doubt that she could go on for ten more, but now she'd met Kal and the only person she wanted to be was herself.

No pretence.

No lies.

Not that she was kidding herself. She knew that if, in the unlikely event that he'd ever met her as 'herself', he wouldn't have even noticed her.

Everything about him was the real deal, from his designer suit to the Rolex on his wrist—no knock-offs for this man. Including women.

The pain of that was a wake-up call far louder, the argument for reality more cogent than any that her boss at the supermarket could make, even using the in-store announcement system.

She had been coasting through her own life, putting all her energies into someone else's, and she would never move on, meet someone who wanted her, the real Lydia Young, unless she started building a life of her own.

'When?' she asked, ungluing her tongue. 'What time?'

Maybe she could throw a sickie, she thought a touch desperately, but instantly rejected the idea as she realised what kind of fuss *that* would cause. This wasn't some anonymous hotel where you could take to your bed and no one would give a damn. And she wasn't some anonymous tourist.

If Lady Rose took to her bed, panic would ensue, doctors would be summoned—probably by helicopter from the capital. And Kal or Dena, probably both, would call Lucy, the Duke of Oldfield and then the game would be up.

No, no, no...

She could do this. She had to do it.

'Relax. She won't be here for a day or two and she won't stay long,' Kal said, not looking at her, but concentrating on serving himself. 'Just for coffee, cake. Dena will arrange everything,' he added, that tiny muscle in his jaw tightening again.

What was that? Tension?

What was his problem?

'Does she speak English? What will we talk about?'

'I believe her English is excellent and I imagine she'll want to talk about your work.'

'Really?' Lydia had a flash image of herself politely explaining the finer points of the checkout scanner to Her Highness over a cup of coffee and had to fight down a hysterical giggle as the world began to unravel around her.

'Play nice,' he said, 'and you'll get a generous donation for one of your good causes.'

Kal's flippancy brought her crashing back to reality. This was not in the least bit funny and her expression must have warned him that she was no more amused by his remark than Rose, whose parents had been killed on a charity mission, would have been.

'I'm sorry, Rose,' he said immediately. 'That was unforgivable.' He shook his head and she realised that for some reason he was as on edge as she was. 'I'm sure she'll just want to talk about Lucy and her grandchildren. It's a while since she's seen them.'

As if that was better!

She'd assumed that being at Bab el Sama would be like staying in a hotel. Great service but everything at a distance. She hadn't anticipated having to live with the pretence of being Rose in this way. This minute by minute deception.

She'd come dangerously, selfishly close to confessing everything to Kal before Dena had interrupted her but she could not, no matter how desperately she wanted to, break Rose's confidence.

She had made this offer with a free heart and couldn't, wouldn't let her down just because that heart wanted to jump ship and fling itself at someone else.

'I appear to have spoiled your appetite,' Kal said, and she took a little heart from the fact that he didn't seem particularly comfortable to hear of their unexpected visitor either.

'I'm good,' she said, picking up her fork and spearing a piece of chicken so succulent that, despite her dry mouth, she had no trouble swallowing it. 'So tell me what, exactly, is your problem, Kal?'

# CHAPTER EIGHT

EXACTLY? Kal took a piece of bread, tore it in two.

'Why would you think I have a problem?' he asked, playing for time in the face of Rose's unexpected challenge.

'There's a muscle just by the corner of your mouth that you'd probably be wise to cover when you play poker,' she replied.

She reached out and touched a spot just below the right hand corner of his mouth.

'Just there.'

As their eyes locked, he kept perfectly still, knowing that if he moved an inch he would be tasting those long, slender fingers, sliding his tongue along the length of each one, and food would be the furthest thing from his mind. That the only thing he'd be eating would be her.

As if sensing the danger, she curled them back into her palm, let her hand drop.

'Should I ever be tempted to gamble, I'll bear that in mind,' he said. Took a mouthful of bread before he blurted out the real reason he had been foisted on her by Lucy and she sent him packing.

Rose made no move to eat, but continued to regard him. 'Well?' she prompted, refusing to let the matter drop. 'I recall that you mentioned your family were personae non gratae at court and presumably, as a royal residence, Bab el Sama is an extension of that. Will Princess Sabirah's visit be awkward for you?'

The breath stopped in his throat. Not suspicion, concern. She was anxious for him...

'This was originally the site of the Khatib tribe's summer camp,' he told her, not sure where exactly he was going with this, but wanting her to understand who, what he was. 'The mountains provided not only water, grazing for the animals, but a fortress at their back in troubled times.' He looked up at the barren peaks towering above them. 'They are impassable.'

'So is that a yes or a no?' she asked, refusing to be diverted by history.

'Good question.'

And the answer was that, far from awkward, Lucy was using court etiquette for his benefit, putting him in a place where his aunt could not, without causing offence to an honoured guest, ignore him.

In London, in her elegant drawing room, it had all seemed so simple. Before he'd met Rose. Now nothing was simple and if this had been for him alone he would have stepped back, taken himself out of the picture for the morning. But this was for his grandfather.

'Maybe you'd better tell me what happened, Kal,' she said when he didn't offer an answer. 'Just enough to stop me from putting my foot in it.'

'Your foot?'

'I'm sorry. You speak such perfect English that I forget that it isn't your first language.' She frowned. 'I'm not even sure what your first language is. Arabic, French...?'

'Take your pick,' he said. 'I grew up speaking both. And quickly added English when my father married for the second time. I know what "putting your foot in it" means. But, to answer your question, the court is wherever the Emir happens to be, so I'm safe enough unless he decides to accompany his wife.'

'And if he does?'

He couldn't get that lucky. Could he? Or was the Emir, like

everyone else, fascinated by this English 'Rose' who'd been orphaned so tragically as a little girl. Who, from the age of sixteen, had taken up her parents' cause, devoted her whole life to the charity they'd founded, adding dozens of other good causes over the years.

'I'm wherever you happen to be, Rose. And you are an honoured guest in his country. Who knows,' he said with a wry smile, 'he might be sufficiently charmed by you to acknowledge my existence.'

'Whoa, whoa…' She put down her fork, sat back. 'Back up, buster. I need to know what I'm getting into here.'

'"Back up, buster"?' he repeated, startled out of his own concerns. 'Where on earth did Lady Rose Napier pick up an expression like that?'

She blinked, appeared to gather herself, physically put the cool façade back in place. 'I meet all kinds of people in my work,' she said. Even her voice had changed slightly, had taken on a hint of steel, as if she was drawing back from him, and he recalled his earlier feeling that she was two separate people. The formal, untouchable, unreadable 'Lady'. And this other woman whose voice was huskier, whose lush mouth was softer, whose eyes seemed to shine a brighter blue. Who used unexpectedly colloquial expressions.

The one he couldn't seem to keep his hands off.

The selfish gene, the one he'd been fighting all his life, urged him to reach out, grasp her hand, stop that Rose from slipping away.

Instead, like her, he took a moment to gather himself, take a step back before, control restored, he said, 'What happened is no secret. Google my family and you'll find enough gossip to fill a book.'

'I'd rather save that for when I've run out of fiction,' she replied crisply. 'The edited highlights will do.'

'I wish it was fiction,' he said. 'My grandfather was hardly a credit to his family.'

He reached for a pitcher of water, offered it to her and, when she nodded, he filled both their glasses.

'Kalil al-Khatib, my grandfather, was the oldest son of the Emir and, although a ruler is free to name his successor, no one ever doubted that it would be him.'

'You have the same name as your grandfather?' she asked.

'It is the tradition. My first son will be named Zaki for my father.' If he achieved recognition, a traditional marriage, a place in the society that had rejected his family.

'That must become rather confusing.'

'Why?'

'Well, if a man has two or three sons, won't all their first-born sons have the same name?' Then, 'Oh, wait. That's why Dena calls you "bin Zaki". That's "son of", isn't it?'

He couldn't stop the smile that betrayed his pleasure. She was so quick, so intelligent, eager to learn.

The curl of desire as, equally pleased with herself for 'getting it', she smiled back.

Then her forehead puckered in a frown as she quickly picked up on what else he'd told her. 'But I don't understand. Why do you call yourself al-Zaki and not al-Khatib?'

'It's a long story,' he said, forcing himself to concentrate on that, rather than the curve of her cheek, the line of her neck. The hollows in her throat that were made for a man's tongue.

'I have all afternoon.'

He sought for a beginning, something that would make sense of tribal history, the harshness of the life, the need for a strong leader.

'My grandfather was his father's favourite. They both loved to ride, hunt in the desert with their falcons. They were, people said, more like twins than father and son. They were both utterly fearless, both much respected. Loved.'

He thought of Dena. She'd called herself his sister, but she was not related to him by blood. Had she loved him, too?

Then, realising that Rose was waiting, 'He was everything that was required of a ruler in those simpler times.'

'Everything?'

'Strong enough to hold off his enemies, to protect the summer grazing, the oases. Keep his people and their stock safe.'

'That would be before the oil?'

He nodded. 'They were still the qualities admired, necessary even in a charismatic leader, but it is true that once the oil started flowing and money began to pour into the country, the role needed a greater vision. Something beyond the warrior, the great hunter, the trusted arbitrator. A man to take the international stage.'

'And your grandfather couldn't adapt?'

'Oh, he adapted,' Kal said wryly. 'Just not in the right way. He was a big man with big appetites and wealth gave him the entire world in which to indulge them. He spent a fortune on a string of racehorses, enjoyed the gaming tables, never lacked some beauty to decorate his arm and, as the heir apparent to one of the new oil rich states, his excesses inevitably attracted media attention. None of it favourable.'

'I bet that went down well at home,' she said with a wry look and he caught again a glimpse of the inner Rose. The one she tried so hard to keep suppressed.

'Like a lead balloon?' he offered.

She laughed, then clapped her hand to her mouth.

'That is the correct expression?' he asked.

'You know it is, Kal.' She shook her head. 'I'm sorry. It's not funny.'

'It all happened a long time ago. My grandfather has long since accepted that he has no one but himself to blame for what happened.'

'So what did happen?' she asked, concentrating on her food rather than looking at him, as if she understood how difficult this was for him. He, on the other hand, watched as she successfully negotiated a second forkful of rice and knew that he could sit here and watch her eat all day.

Instead, he followed her example, picking up a piece of fish, forcing himself to concentrate on the story.

'In an attempt to remind Kalil of his duty,' he went on, 'encourage him to return home and settle down, his family arranged his marriage to the daughter of one of the most powerful tribal elders.'

'Arranged?' He caught the slightly disparaging lift of her eyebrows, the sideways glance.

'It is how it is done, Rose. To be accepted as the husband of a precious daughter is to be honoured. And an alliance, ties of kinship between families, adds strength in times of trouble.'

'Very useful when it comes to hanging on to land, I imagine. Especially when it lies over a vast oilfield. Does the girl get a say at all?'

'Of course,' he said.

'But who would refuse the man who was going to be Emir?'

'Marriage binds tribal societies together, Rose. I'm not saying that ours is an infallible system, but everyone has a stake in the partnership succeeding. No one wants to match two young people who will be unhappy.'

'Yours?'

She sounded sceptical. He could see why she might be. He was the second generation to be born and live his entire life in Europe. But at heart...

'There's no place for love?'

'That would be the happy-ever-after fairy tale perpetrated by Hollywood?' he responded irritably.

He'd hoped that she would understand. Then, remembering Lucy's concern that she was being guided towards marriage not of her own choice, he realised that she probably did understand rather more than most. And found himself wondering just how much choice a girl really had in a society where being married to a powerful man was the ideal. When her family's fortune might rise or fall on her decision.

'Hollywood came rather late in the story, Kal. Ever heard

of Shakespeare? "Love is not love, Which alters when it altera-
tion finds, Or bends with the remover to remove: Oh, no! it is
an ever-fixéd mark, That looks on tempests and is never shaken;
It is the star to every wandering bark…"'

She said the words with such passion, such belief, that a stab
of longing pierced him and for a moment he couldn't breathe.
Wanted to believe that out of an entire world it was possible
for two people to find one another. Reach out and with the
touch of a hand make a commitment that would last a lifetime.

Knowing it for nonsense, that anyone who believed in it was
going to get hurt, he shook his head.

'It's the same story for the same gullible audience,' he
replied. That kind of attraction is no more than sexual chemistry. Powerful, undoubtedly, but short-lived. 'I've lived with
the aftermath of "love" all my life, Rose. The hurt, the disillu-
sion. The confused children.'

She reached out, laid her hand over his. 'I'm sorry.' Then,
as swiftly she removed it. 'I didn't think.'

He shrugged. 'I admit that my family is an extreme case,'
he said, but how could he ever put his trust in such here today,
gone tomorrow feelings? He'd much rather leave the matter to
wiser heads. 'Not that it was a problem in my grandfather's
case. His response to the summons home for the formal be-
trothal was a front page appearance on every newspaper with
his new bride, a glamorous British starlet who was, he swore,
the love of his life.'

'Ouch!' she said. Then, her face softening, 'But how romantic.'

'The romance was, without doubt, intense…' 'Like a
rocket', was the way his grandfather had described it. Hot,
fast, spectacular and gone as quickly as the coloured stars
faded from the sky. 'But the reason for the swift marriage was
rather more prosaic. She was pregnant.'

'Oh.'

'He knew his father would be angry, his chosen bride's
family outraged, but, universally popular and always a favour-

ite, he was confident that the birth of a son would bring him forgiveness.'

'I take it he was mistaken.'

'When a favoured son falls from grace it's a very long drop, Rose.'

'So his father disinherited him.'

'Not immediately. He was told his new bride was not welcome in Ramal Hamrah, but that when he was prepared to settle down he could come home. My grandfather wasn't a man to abandon his bride and return like a dog with his tail between his legs.'

'I like him for that.'

'Everyone likes him, Rose. That was part of the problem.'

'And you,' she said gently. 'You love him.'

'He is my *jaddi'l habeeb,*' he told her. 'My beloved grand-father. While my own father was following in his father's foot-steps, *Jaddi* taught me to speak Arabic, the stories of my people. Their history.'

'And he gave it all up for love.'

'While his studious, dutiful younger brother soothed outraged sensibilities and rescued his father's tattered pride by marrying the girl chosen for the heir. Within a year he had a son with blood that could be traced back a thousand years and was visibly putting all this new found wealth to work for his father's people.'

'A new man for a new age.'

'Smarter than my grandfather, certainly. When his father had a stroke *Jaddi* raced home, but he was too late. The Emir had slipped into a coma and was beyond extending the hand of for-giveness. There was to be no feast for the prodigal.'

'Poor man.'

He glanced at her, uncertain who she was referring to.

'I wonder if there was a moment when he knew it was too late. The Emir. Wished he had acted differently? You think that you have all the time in world to say the words. When my father was killed I wanted to tell him…'

She broke off, unable to continue, and it was his turn to reach out for her hand, curl his fingers around it, hold tight as she remembered the family that had been torn from her.

After a moment she shook her head. 'I'm fine, Kal.'

Was she? He'd never lost anyone close to him. Rose had only her grandfather and he wished he could share his many grandparents, parents, siblings with her.

'What did you want to tell him, Rose?' he pressed, wanting to know about her. How she felt. What her life had been like.

'That I loved him,' she said. And for a moment her eyes were noticeably brighter. 'He used to take me for walks in the wood on Sunday mornings. Show me things. The names of trees, flowers, birds.'

'Your mother didn't go with you?'

She shook her head. 'She stayed at home and cooked lunch but we'd always look for something special to take home for her. A big shiny conker or a bird's feather or a pretty stone.'

The Marchioness slaving over a hot stove? An unlikely image, but Rose's mother hadn't been born to the purple. She'd qualified as a doctor despite the odds, had met her polo playing Marquess in A&E when he'd taken a tumble from his horse.

Such ordinary domesticity must evoke a genuine yearning in the breast of a young woman who'd been brought up by a starchy old aristocrat who probably didn't even know where the kitchen was.

'I should have told him every day how much I loved him. That's all there is in the end, Kal. Love. Nothing else matters.'

'It's tragic that you had so little time to get to know him. Be with him. With both of them,' he said. 'To lose a mother so young… What do you remember about her?'

She started, as if brought back from some distant place, then said, 'Her bravery, determination. How much she loved my father.'

She looked at her hand, clasped in his, reclaimed it.

'Go on with your story, Kal,' she urged.

He didn't want to talk about his family. He wanted to know more about her. His six-year-old memories of his mother were of stories, treats, hugs. Were Rose's most abiding memories really of her mother's bravery? Or was that the result of years of media brainwashing?

'What happened after your great-grandfather died?' she pressed.

There was definitely something wrong here, he could sense it, but Rose Napier was no more than a means to an end, he reminded himself. She was not his concern.

'When *Jaddi* learned that his father had named his younger brother as Emir his heart broke, not just with grief,' he told her, refocusing himself on what was important, 'but with guilt, too. For a while he was crazy.'

He stared at the plate in front of him. Somehow, he'd managed to clear it, although he hadn't tasted a thing.

'What happened?' she pressed. 'What did he do?'

'He refused to swear allegiance to his younger brother, raised disaffected tribes in the north, attacked the citadel. He thought that the people would rise to him, but he'd been away for a long time. While they'd once adored the dashing young sheikh, in his absence they had grown to admire and respect his brother.'

'Was anyone hurt?'

He shook his head. 'When it was obvious that he lacked popular support, his allies were quick to make their peace with the man holding the purse strings.'

'It's like something out of a Shakespearean tragedy,' she said.

'I suppose it is. But it was of his own making. Even then, if he'd been prepared to acknowledge his brother as ruler, publicly bow the knee, he would have been allowed to stay. Play his part. When he refused to humiliate himself in that way, his brother exiled him from the tribe, stripped him of his name, title, banished him. All he was left with was the financial settlement that his father had hoped would compensate him for being supplanted by his younger brother.'

'And your father? Was he included in this p...

'Banishment was for *Jaddi* alone, but the res...
a father does not bear the name of his tribe, the tit...
him by birth...'

'So you are al-Zaki.'

'A name without history,' he said. Without honour. 'My father and I are free to come and go, as is my sister. I have an office, an apartment in Rumaillah but, without a family, I remain invisible.' His letters returned unanswered. Barred from his place in the *majlis*. Forbidden any way of appealing for mercy for a dying man. Reduced to using this woman.

'What do you think will happen when Princess Sabirah comes here? Will she "see" you?' she asked.

'Don't worry about it,' he said, angry with himself, angry with the Emir, angry with her for making him feel guilty. 'Her Highness won't do anything to embarrass her distinguished guest.'

That was what Lucy was relying on, anyway. If she acknowledged him, he would beg her to intercede with the Emir for his grandfather. That was all that was left, he thought bitterly. A chance to plead with the woman who shared the Emir's pillow to show pity on a dying man.

Lydia felt the emptiness in Kal's words, the loss, an underlying anger too, but to say that she was sorry would be meaningless and so she said nothing—she'd already said far too much, come close to blowing the whole deal.

The silence drifted back, broken only by the clink of dishes when Yatimah appeared to clear the table, loading everything on to the tray.

Having come—in a moment of high emotion—perilously close to letting slip the truth about her own father's death, she took the chance to gather herself before turning to Yatimah to thank her for the meal.

'*La shokr ala wageb, sitti.* No thanks are due for duty.'

'Will you say that again?' Lydia begged, grabbing the

ce to move away from dangerous territory. Listening carefully and repeating it after her self-appointed teacher.

'I will bring coffee?'

*'Nam. Shukran.'*

When she'd gone, Kal said, 'You listen well, Rose.'

'I try to pick up a few words of the local language when I'm on holiday. Even if it's only hello and thank you.' The truth, and how good that felt, but before he could ask where she usually went on holiday, 'So, what time are we going fishing?'

'Maybe we should give that a miss today,' he said. 'Wait until you're really bored.'

She tried not to look too happy about that.

'You might have a long wait. I've got the most beautiful garden to explore, a swimming pool to lie beside and a stack of good books to read. In fact, as soon as we've had coffee I'll decide which to do first.'

*'Qahwa.* The Arabic for coffee is *qahwa.* You make the q sound in the back of your throat.'

*'Ga howa?'*

'Perfect.' Then, with one of those slow smiles that sent a dangerous finger of heat funnelling through her, 'Maybe we should add Arabic lessons to the schedule.'

Doing her best to ignore it, she said, 'You do know that I had planned to simply lie in the sun for a week?'

'You can listen, speak lying down, can't you?'

Lydia tried to block out the image of Kal, stretched out on a lounger beside her at the pool she'd glimpsed from the dining room, his skin glistening in the sun while he attempted to teach her the rudiments of a language he clearly loved.

Did he really believe that she would be able to concentrate?

'Lying in the sun resting,' she elaborated swiftly, all the emphasis on *resting.* 'You seem determined to keep me permanently occupied. Rushing around, doing stuff.'

'It won't be hard work, I promise you.'

His low honeyed voice promised her all kinds of things,

none of them arduous, and as he picked up her hand the heat intensified.

'We can begin with something simple.' And, never taking his eyes from her face, he touched his lips to the tip of her little finger. '*Wahid.*'

'*Wahid?*'

'One.'

'*Ithnan.*' His lips moved on to her ring finger, lingered while she attempted to hold her wits together and repeat the word.

'*Ithnan.* Two.'

'*Thalatha.*'

Something inside her was melting and it took her so long to respond that he began to nibble on the tip of her middle finger.

'*Thalatha!*'

'*Arba'a.*' And he drove home the message with four tiny kisses on the tip, the first joint, the second joint, the knuckle of her forefinger.

'*Arba'a.*' It was her bones that were the problem, she decided. Her bones were melting. That was why she couldn't move. Pull free. 'Four.'

'*Khamsa.*' He looked for a moment at her thumb, then took the length of it in his mouth before slowly pulling back to the tip. 'Five.'

He was right. This was a language lesson she was never going to forget. She mindlessly held out her other hand so that he could teach her the numbers six to ten, already anticipating the continuation of a lesson involving every part of her body.

He did not take it and, catching her breath as she came back to earth, she used it to sweep her hair behind her ear, managing a very creditable, '*Shukran,* Kal.'

Yatimah placed a tray containing a small brass coffee pot and tiny cups on the table beside her.

Feeling ridiculously light-headed as she realised that he must have seen her coming, that he had not rejected her but chosen discretion, she said, 'Truly, that was a huge improvement on Mrs Latimer's Year Six French class.'

'Mrs Latimer?' Lucy had been saying something about Rose not being allowed to go to school when he'd interrupted her. He wished now he'd been less impatient...

For a moment Lydia's mind froze.

'A t-tutor,' she stuttered as Kal continued to look at her, a frown creasing that wide forehead.

She longed to tell him everything. Tell him about her brave mother who'd lost her husband and her mobility in one tragic moment on an icy road. Tell him about school, how she'd left when she was sixteen because what was the point of staying on when she would never have left her mother to go away to university? Tell him everything...

She was rescued from his obvious suspicion by the beep of a text arriving on her mobile phone.

'Excuse me,' she said, retrieving it from her pocket. 'It might be...' She swallowed, unable to say the word *grandfather,* turned away to check it, assuming that it was simply a 'have fun' response from her mother to her own text.

But it wasn't from her mother. It was from Rose.

*Vtl you b on frnt pge am!*

*Vital you be on the front page tomorrow morning...*

Lydia swallowed. Had she been recognised? Clearly she had to convince someone that she really was in Bab el Sama.

She quickly keyed in *OK* and hit 'send', returning the phone to her pocket. Realised that Kal was watching her intently.

'Is there a problem?' he asked as Yatimah offered them each a cup, then filled them with a thin straw-coloured aromatic liquid that was nothing like any coffee she'd ever seen.

'Good heavens, no!' she said with a nervous laugh which, even to her own ears, rang about as true as a cracked bell.

Only him.

Only her guilt that she was lying to a man who made her feel things that needed total honesty. And she couldn't be honest. The text was a timely reminder just how deeply she was embedded in this pretence. She was doing this for Rose and right now only she mattered...

They were four hours ahead of London, plenty of time to make the morning papers, but to accomplish that she had to get into the open in daylight. On her own. Wearing as little as possible.

She and Rose both knew that what the paparazzi were really hoping for was a picture of her in a private 'love nest' scenario with Rupert Devenish.

That was never going to happen, so in order to keep them focused, they'd planned a slow striptease to keep those lenses on her for the entire week.

First up would be a walk along the beach in shorts with a shirt open over a bathing suit.

After that she was going to discard the shirt to reveal a bathing suit top beneath it. Rare enough to excite interest, but nothing particularly sensational—it was a very demure bathing suit. Finally she'd strip down to the swimsuit. That should be enough to keep the photographers on their toes, but there was a bikini in reserve in case of unforeseen emergencies.

Rose's text suggested they were in the 'unforeseen emergency' category. What she didn't, couldn't know was that her good friend Lucy al-Khatib had provided her with a 'protector'. Kal was relaxed about letting her wander, unseen by the outside world, in the shelter of the gardens, but she very much doubted that he'd sit back and let her take a walk along the beach without her minder.

While it was true that his presence would absolutely guarantee a front page spot, she also recognised that the presence of some unknown man in close attendance would cause more problems than it solved.

She was going to have to evade her watchdog and get down to the beach and she had less than an hour in which to manage it.

Kal watched Rose sip gingerly at the scalding coffee. Clearly, whatever had been in the text had not been good news.

The colour had drained from her face and a man didn't have to be fluent in body language to see that she was positively twitching to get away.

Which begged the question, why didn't she just say, *Great lunch, see you later...* and walk away? Or tell him that something had come up that she had to deal with?

Why was she sitting there like a cat on hot bricks, doing her best to pretend that nothing was wrong?

A gentleman would make it easy for her. Make an excuse himself and leave her to get on with whatever it was she wanted to do.

A man who'd been charged with her safety, in the face of some unspecified threat, would be rather less obliging. Lucy might have disparaged the Duke's concerns, but she hadn't dismissed them entirely.

She hadn't elaborated on them, either. Could it be that she was more worried about what Rose might do than what some imaginary assailant had in mind?

Maybe he should give her a call right now. Except that would leave Rose on her own, which didn't seem like a great idea.

'This is desert coffee,' he said conversationally. 'The beans are not ground but boiled whole with cardamom seeds. For the digestion.'

'Really? It's different. Very good,' she said, although he doubted she had even tasted it.

As she put the cup down, clearly eager to be away, he said, 'Traditionally, politeness requires that you drink two cups.'

'Two?'

She scarcely managed to hide her dismay and his concern deepened. What on earth had been in that text?

'They're very small. If you hold out the cup, like this,' he said, holding out his own cup, 'Yatimah will refill it for you.'

Obediently she held out the cup. Drank it as quickly as she could without scalding her mouth, handed the cup back to the girl.

And it was refilled a third time.

'She'll refill it as often as you hold it out like that,' he explained. 'When you've had enough you have to shake the cup from side to side to indicate that you have had enough.'

'Oh. Right.' She swallowed it down, shook the cup the way he told her, thanked Yatimah who, at a look from him, quickly disappeared. Rose, looking as if she wanted to bolt after her, said, 'If you'll excuse me, Kal, I'll go and get my book. Find somewhere quiet to read. You don't have to stand guard over me while I do that, do you?'

'Not if you stay within the garden,' he said, rising to his feet, easing back her chair.

'What about the beach?' she asked, so casually that he knew that was where she would be heading the minute he took his eyes off her. 'That's private, isn't it?'

'It's private in that no one will come ashore and have a picnic. Local people respect the privacy of the Emir and his guests, but the creek is busy.' He glanced across the water. 'There are plenty of boats where a photographer hoping to catch a candid shot of you could hide out.' He turned back to her. 'Lucy said you found the intrusion stressful but if you want to risk a walk along the shore, I'll be happy to accompany you.'

'Lady Rose Napier plus unknown man on a beach? Now, that really would make their day.' Her laughter lacked any real suggestion of amusement. 'I'll stick to the garden, thanks.' Then, 'Why don't you take yourself off on that fishing trip you're so keen on? Give me a break from the maggots.'

Give her a break? Where on earth had the secluded Lady Rose picked up these expressions?

'The maggots will be disappointed,' he said, coming up with a smile. 'I'll see you at dinner?'

'Of course.'

Her relief was palpable at the prospect of an entire afternoon free of him. He would have been offended but, from the way she'd responded to his kisses, he knew it wasn't personal.

'Although I'd better put in a few laps at the pool, too, or at this rate none of the clothes I brought with me will fit.'

'There's an upside to everything,' he replied.

His reward was a hot blush before she lifted her hand in a small, oddly awkward, see-you-later gesture and walked quickly towards the cottage.

Kal, getting the message loud and clear, didn't move until she was out of sight.

# CHAPTER NINE

LYDIA'S luggage had been unpacked and put away and she quickly hunted through drawers, doing her best not to linger and drool over silk, cashmere, finest linen, as she searched for a swimsuit.

She had refused to accept a penny from Rose for this assignment. This was a labour of love, gratitude, respect and she'd insisted on taking a week of her paid holiday entitlement. But Rose had found a way to reward her anyway. She'd raided her wardrobe for more clothes than she could possibly wear in a week at the beach. Clothes she had never worn. Insisting that Lydia keep them.

The half a dozen swimsuits that she'd packed, each bearing the name of a world famous designer, were uniformly gorgeous. Each, inevitably, had the 'pink rose' theme and Lydia chose a striking black one-piece costume with a single long-stemmed rose embroidered across the front from the right hip, with stem and leaves curling diagonally across the stomach, so that the bud bloomed above her heart.

It was clearly a one-off that had been made especially for her and, with luck, the delighted designer would call the gossip pages and claim whatever PR was going. Which would help to establish that it could be no one but Rose on the Bab el Sama beach.

It fitted her like a glove, holding, lifting in all the right places. She didn't waste any time admiring her reflection, however, but threw the kaftan over it, ran a brush through her hair, freshened her lipstick and grabbed a book.

All she had to do now was find her way down to the beach unobserved and, avoiding the exit through the garden room to the terrace where Kal might still be lingering, she slipped out through the dining room.

Kal stood in the dark shadows at the top of a rocky outcrop, sweeping the water with a pair of powerful glasses, hoping to pick up anything out of place. Anyone who didn't have business on the water.

It was as peaceful a scene as a bodyguard could hope for. Fishermen, traders, local people pottering on their boats.

He glanced at his watch, wondering how much longer Rose would be. Because she'd come. He'd put money on it. But why?

He took out his BlackBerry and put Rose's name into the search engine. There was a picture of her leaving the lunch yesterday, '…radiant…' as she left for a week in Bab el Sama. Raising the question of whether she'd be alone.

There were other photographs. One of her with Rupert Devenish a couple of weeks earlier. Not looking radiant.

Maybe she had just been tired. Or perhaps the hollows in her cheeks, around her eyes were the result of a cold or a headache. Perhaps the camera angle was unflattering. Whatever it was, she had none of the glow that had reached out, grabbed him by the throat and refused to let go.

In fact she looked like a pale imitation of his Rose. He continued his search for answers until the soft slap of leather thongs against the stone steps warned him that she was on her way. He could have told her that to be silent she would need to remove her shoes. But then she hadn't expected him to be there.

She paused in a deep patch of shade at the bottom of the steps that led from the garden, a book in one hand, presumably an alibi in case he hadn't done as she'd suggested and conveniently removed himself from the scene, but instead taken his promise to Lucy seriously enough to stick around and keep an eye on her.

He kept very still as she looked around, checking that the beach was empty. Even if she had looked up, he was well hidden from the casual glance, but she was only concerned that the beach was empty and, having made certain the coast was clear, she put the book on the step. Then she took the mobile phone from her pocket and placed it on top.

No…

The word stilled on his lips as she reached back and pulled the kaftan over her head to reveal a simple one-piece black swimsuit that displayed every curve, every line of her body to perfection. A slender neck, circled with a fine gold chain on which hung a rosebud pendant. Wide, elegant shoulders, an inviting cleavage that hadn't appeared on the photograph of her in the evening gown. A proper waist, gently flared hips and then those endless legs, perfect ankles, long slender feet.

For a moment she stood there, as if summoning up the courage to carry on.

Don't…

The thought of his Rose appearing on the front page of tomorrow's papers in a swimsuit, her body being leered at by millions of men, was utterly abhorrent to him and he knew that the rush of protectiveness he felt had nothing whatever to do with the charge that Lucy had laid on him.

He'd spent much of his life on beaches, around swimming pools with women who would have raised their sophisticated eyebrows at such a puritan reaction and he knew his response was the very worst kind of double standard.

By modern standards, the costume she was wearing was modest.

Before he could move, do anything, she draped the kaftan over a low branch and she stepped into the sun. Shoulders back, head high, she walked towards the water, where she paused to scan the creek.

The light breeze caught her hair, lifting tiny strands that caught the light, lending her an ethereal quality.

Dear God, she was beautiful.

As cool and mysterious as a princess in some *Arabian Nights* story, escaped from some desperate danger and washed up on an unknown shore, waiting for Sinbad to rescue her, restore her to her prince.

'That's enough,' he whispered. 'Turn back now. Come back to me.'

She glanced round, looking up, as if she'd heard him, but it was a bird quartering the air that had caught her attention and, having watched it for a moment, she turned, then took a step...

'No!'

...bent to pick up something from the sand. It was a piece of sand-polished glass and, as she held it up to the light, he caught an echo of the flash out on the creek.

He lifted the glasses, scanned the water and this time found the telltale glint as the sunlight dancing on the water was reflected off a lens hidden beneath a tarpaulin on an anonymous-looking motor launch. It was anchored amongst half a dozen or so boats on the far side of the creek, its name obscured, deliberately, he had no doubt, and he had to fight the urge to race after Rose, drag her back.

But the one thing they were in complete agreement about was that she must not be photographed with him.

It would provoke a feeding frenzy among the press and it wouldn't take them five minutes to uncover his identity. His entire history would be rehashed in the press, along with the playboy lifestyle of both his grandfather and father, to fuel innuendo-laden speculation about why he was in Bab el Sama with Rose.

And no one was going to believe that the millionaire CEO of an international air freight business had accompanied Lady Rose Napier to Bab el Sama as her bodyguard. The millionaire grandson of an exiled sheikh, son of an international playboy, he hadn't been exactly short of media coverage himself before he'd stopped the drift. Found a purpose in life.

The fallout from that would cause a lot more embarrassment than even the most revealing photograph.

Worse, her grandfather, the Duke, would be apoplectic and blame Lucy for embroiling her in such a mess. Not to mention the fact that the Emir would be so angry that Kalil could kiss goodbye forever to any chance of *Jaddi*'s banishment being lifted so that he could die in peace at Umm al Sama.

His sole remit was to protect Lady Rose from danger. Shooting her with a camera didn't count, especially when she was going out of her way to make it easy for whoever was laid up in that boat.

He watched her as, apparently oblivious to scrutiny from both sea and shore, she wandered along the shoreline, stopping now and then to pick up a shell or a pebble. Lifting a hand to push back her hair. It was a classic image, one he knew that picture editors around the world would lap up, putting their own spin on it in a dozen headlines, most of them including the word *alone*.

So who had sent the message that had her scurrying to expose herself to the world's press?

He looked down at the shady step where she'd left her phone.

Lydia stood for a moment at the edge of the water, lifting her face to the sun, the gorgeous feeling of wet sand seeping between her toes taking her back to childhood holidays when her father had been alive, memories of her mother laughing as the waves caught her.

She remembered one holiday when she'd collected a whole bucket full of shells. By the end of their stay, they had smelled so bad that her father had refused to put them in the car. To stop her tears at the loss of her treasures, her mother had washed the most special one, given her a heart-shaped box to keep it in.

She still had her memory box. It contained a picture of

her father, laughing as she splashed him with a hosepipe. Her mother with the world famous couturier she'd worked for before the accident. The newspaper picture of her in the very first 'Lady Rose' outfit her mother had made when she was fifteen.

There had been a rush of additions in that brief spell when she'd thought she was in love. All but one of those had been tossed away with many more tears than the shells when she'd realised the truth. She'd kept just one thing, a theatre programme, because all memories were important. Even the bad ones. If you didn't remember, you didn't learn...

After that the memories had nearly all involved her looka-like gigs. Her life as someone else.

Looking around, she saw the edge of an oyster shell sticking out of sand washed clean by the receding tide.

She bent to ease it out, rinsed it off in the water, turned it over to reveal the pink and blue iridescence of mother-of-pearl. A keepsake to remind her of this moment, this beach, Kal al-Zaki kissing her fingers as he taught her Arabic numbers. A memory to bring out when she was old and all this would seem like a dream that had happened to someone else.

The last one she'd ever put in that old box, she vowed. She was never going to do this again, be Rose. It was time to start living her own life, making her own memories. No more pretence.

She stood for a moment, holding the shell, uncertain which way to go. Then, choosing to have the wind in her face, she turned right, towards the sea, wishing that Kal was walking with her to point out the landmarks, tell her the story behind a crumbling tower on the highest point on the far bank. To hold her hand as she turned through the curve that had taken Kal out of sight that morning.

Until now Kal had been able to dismiss the turmoil induced by his charge as nothing more than the natural response of a healthy male for a woman who had hit all the right buttons.

He was thirty-three, had been surrounded by beautiful women all his life and was familiar with desire in all its guises, but as he'd got older, become more certain what he wanted, he'd found it easy to stay uninvolved.

That he'd been knocked so unexpectedly sideways by Lady Rose Napier was, he'd been convinced, no more than the heightened allure of the unobtainable.

All that went out of the window in the moment she stepped out of his sight.

Lydia continued for as long as she dared, scanning the creek, hoping for some sign that there was someone out there.

Then, because she doubted it would be long before someone realised that she wasn't where she was meant to be and start looking for her, she turned back, relieved to be picking her way across the soft sand to the shade, the anonymity of the giant rock formation near the foot of the steps.

She'd half expected to find Yatimah standing guard over her book, her phone, her expression disapproving, but her escapade had gone unobserved. Relieved, she pushed her feet into the leather thong sandals, then turned to carefully lift the kaftan from the branch.

It wasn't there and she looked down to see if it had fallen.

Took a step into the shadows behind the rocks, assuming that it had been caught by a gust of wind and blown there.

And another.

Without warning, she was seized from behind around the waist, lifted clear of the sand, her body held tight against the hard frame of a man.

As she struggled to get free, she pounded at the arm holding her, using the edge of the shell as a weapon, opened her mouth to scream.

A hand cut off the sound.

'Looking for something, Lady Rose?'

She stilled. Kal…

She'd known it even before he'd spoken. Knew that woody scent. Would always know it...

As soon as she stopped struggling he dropped his hand and, knowing he was going to be mad at her, she got in first with, 'I thought you were going fishing.'

'And I thought you were going to curl up by the pool with a good book.'

He set her down and, with the utmost reluctance, she turned to face him.

'I am.' Head up. And Lady Rose, the Duke's granddaughter at her most aristocratic, she added, 'I decided to take a detour.'

'And give one of your paparazzi army tomorrow's front page picture?'

She instinctively glanced at the phone lying defenceless on top of her book. 'Have you been reading my messages?' she demanded.

'No need. You've just told me everything I need to know.'

'No...'

'What is it, Rose?' he asked. 'Are you a publicity junkie? Can't you bear to see an entire week go by without your picture on the front page?'

She opened her mouth to protest. Closed it again.

His anger was suppressed, but there was no doubting how he felt at being deceived, made a fool of, and who could blame him? Except, of course, he hadn't. He'd been ahead of her every step of the way. Instead, she shook her head, held up her hands.

'You've got me, Kal. Bang to rights.' She took a step back. 'Can I have my dress back now?'

As he reached up, lifted the kaftan down from the place he'd hidden it, she saw the blood oozing from his arm where she'd slashed at him with the shell she was still clutching.

She dropped it as if it burned, reached out to him, drew back without touching him. She'd lied to him and he knew it.

'I hurt you,' she said helplessly.

He glanced at the wound she'd made, shrugged. 'Nothing that I didn't ask for.'

'Maybe, but it still needs cleaning.' Ignoring the dress he was holding out to her, she began to run up the steps. 'Sea shells have all kinds of horrible things in them,' she said. 'You can get septicaemia.'

'Is that right?'

Realising that he hadn't followed her, she stopped, looked back. 'Truly.' Then, realising that perhaps that wasn't the best choice of word, 'I've been on a first aid course.' She offered her hand but, when he didn't take it, said, 'Please, Kal.'

Relenting, he slung the dress over his shoulder, stooped to pick up the book and phone she'd abandoned in her rush to heal, adding the number of his mobile phone to her contact list. Adding hers to his as he followed her up to the house, the bedroom where he'd left her sleeping a few hours earlier, into the huge, luxurious bathroom beyond.

'I've put my number in your phone,' he said, putting them on a table. 'In case you should ever need it.'

She rolled her eyes. 'Sit there!'

He obediently settled himself on a wide upholstered bench while she took a small first aid box from a large cupboard that was filled with the cosmetics and toiletries she'd brought with her and searched through it for sachets containing antiseptic wipes.

'Why did you do it?' He addressed the top of her head as she bent over him, cleaning up the scratches she'd made.

'This is nothing,' she said. 'I did a self-defence course and you're really lucky I wasn't wearing high heels.'

'I wasn't referring to your attempt to chop my arm off. Why did you strip off for that photographer?'

'I didn't strip off!' she declared, so flustered by the accusation that for a moment she forgot what she was doing. Then, getting a grip, 'I took a walk on the beach in a swimsuit. A very modest swimsuit.'

Modest by today's standards, maybe, but this close, clinging like a second skin, revealing perhaps more than she realised, as she bent over him—suggesting more—the effect was far more enticing than an entire beach filled with topless lovelies.

She looked up. 'Did you say "photographer"?'

'I did.'

She straightened abruptly as she saw exactly where his eyes were focused.

'You saw him?'

'He was in a launch out on the creek and well camouflaged from above. He forgot about the sun reflecting off the water.'

The tension went out of her shoulders, her neck. Relief, he thought. That was sheer relief.

'So why did you do it?' he persisted.

'I thought we'd established that,' she said, concentrating once more on his arm.

The speed with which she'd grabbed at the insulting explanation he'd offered suggested desperation to hide the real reason for her exhibitionism. While he had his own suspicions, he was beginning to wish he'd overcome his squeamishness about plundering her phone for the answer.

'Maybe you'd better run it by me again.'

Apparently satisfied with the clean up job on his arm, or maybe just wanting to put a little distance between them, she gathered up the used wipes, dropped them in a bin.

'It's a game, Kal,' she said, busying herself, filling a marble basin with warm water. Looking anywhere but at him. 'We need each other. Celebrities need headlines, the media have an insatiable appetite for stories. The trick is to give them what they want and then hope they'll leave you alone.'

She plunged her hands in the water, then looked around for soap.

He took a piece from a crystal bowl but did not hand it to her. Instead, he put his arms around her, trapping her as he leaned into her back, his chin against her hair as he dipped his hands into the water and began to soap her fingers.

'Kal!' she protested, but feebly. They both knew she wasn't going anywhere until she'd told him what was going on.

'What, exactly, do they want from you?' he asked.

'Right now?' The words came out as a squeak and he waited while she took a breath. 'Right now,' she repeated, 'they'd give their eye teeth for a picture of me here, in flagrante with Rupert Devenish.' She tried a laugh, attempting to ignore the way his thumb was circling her palm. The way she was relaxing against him. 'He's—'

'I read the newspapers,' he said, not wanting to hear the words on her lips. Or that it was Lucy who'd filled him in on the marriage mania in the gossip columns. 'But that isn't going to happen, is it?'

Unless he'd got it totally wrong and the text had been from Devenish announcing his imminent arrival, urging Rose to convince the paparazzi that she was alone before he joined her.

In which case her eager response to him, the way she had softened in the circle of his arms, surrendered her hands for him to do with what he would, was going to take a little—make that a lot of—explaining.

'It's not going to happen,' she confirmed. 'I'm afraid they're going to have to make do with the clichéd Lady Rose, alone on a beach, how sad, picture.'

And it was his turn to feel the tension slide away from his shoulders.

But only halfway.

According to Lucy, Rose was falling apart because of the constant intrusion into her life. Ten years without being able to lift a finger unobserved, she'd said.

He wasn't getting that impression from Rose. Far from it. She seemed totally relaxed about what could only be construed as a unwarranted intrusion into her private life.

'And if they aren't?' he asked.

A tiny tremor rippled through her and he knew that there was a lot more to this than she was telling him.

'Trust me, Rose,' he said. 'The picture will be a sensation.' He reached for a towel, taking her hands, drying them one finger at a time. Then, because he was still angry with her, 'And if I'm wrong you can always go for the topless option tomorrow.'

'Tomorrow will be too late...'

She caught herself, no doubt realising that she should have objected to the 'topless', not the 'tomorrow'. But he had the answer to at least one of his questions.

For some reason she wanted a picture of herself on the front page and for some reason it had to be tomorrow. And he went straight back to that mysterious threat.

Was this what it was all about? Give me a photograph or... Or what?

What on earth could anyone have over the universally loved and admired 'people's angel'?

Except, of course, that the woman in his arms was not Rose Napier.

On some subconscious level he'd known that from the moment she'd walked into the VIP lounge at the airport. Right from the beginning, he'd sensed the split personality, the separation between the woman playing a role—and occasionally slipping—and the woman who shone through the disguise, lighting him up not just like a rocket, but the whole damn fourth of July scenario. Whoosh, bang, the sky filled with coloured stars.

He didn't trust it, knew it was a temporary aberration, nothing but chemistry, but he finally understood why his grandfather had lost his head, lost his country over a woman.

He was here on a one-off last-chance mission and from the moment she'd appeared on the scene this woman had attacked all his systems like a virus taking over a computer memory, supplanting herself in place of everything that was vital, important, real.

Lucy had obviously told him a pack of lies—he was only here to inveigle his way into a meeting with Princess Sabirah, so why would he be bothered with something as important as the truth?

Presumably the real Rose was holed up in some private love nest with Rupert while this woman, this lovely woman who was superficially so like her, was nothing but a plant to keep the press focused on Bab el Sama.

So what had gone wrong? Had someone found out? Threatened to expose the switch? Directing his own personal photo shoot by text?

In which case he had no doubt that the topless scenario would be the next demand. Because, even if she was a fake, that picture would be worth millions to the photographer who delivered it to a picture agency.

'You've got nothing to worry about,' he said, tossing the towel aside, not sure who he was most angry with, Lucy or this woman, whoever she was, for putting at risk his own mission.

No, that was wrong. Lucy had used the situation to give him a chance. This woman had lit him up, responding to his kisses as if he was the last man on earth. Lies, lies, lies...

'I guarantee you that there won't be a picture editor in London who won't grab that picture of you for their front page tomorrow.'

Her all too obvious relief flipped something in his brain and he stroked the pad of his thumb over the exquisite rose that curved invitingly across her breast in an insultingly intimate gesture, opened his mouth over her all too obvious response as the bud beneath the costume leapt to his touch.

Her throat moved as she swallowed, doing her best to ignore the intimacy of his touch, but the tiny shiver that rippled through her betrayed pleasure, desire, need and her response was not to pull away but buckle against him.

Too late, he discovered that he was the one caught in a lie, because it didn't matter who she was, he desired her as he had never desired any other woman. Not just with his body, but with his heart, his soul and simply holding her was not enough.

Nothing could disguise from her how very much it wasn't enough but, as the wildfire of desire swept through him, he was not alone. Her seeking lips found his neck, trailed moist kisses across his chin, touched his lips, her need as desperate as his.

'Whoever you are,' he murmured, looking down at her, 'you can trust me on that…'

For a moment she looked at him, her mouth soft, her lids heavy with desire and the slow-burning fuse, lit in the moment their eyes had first met, of that unfinished kiss, lay between them.

The air was heavy with the desire of two people for whom the need to touch, to explore, to be one, blotted out memory, bypassed hard-learned lessons, destroyed reason.

Lydia heard him, understood what he was saying, but wrapped in the powerful arms of a man she desired beyond sense, this was not a time for questions, answers. Time was suspended. There was no past, no future. This was for now. Only the senses survived—scent, taste, touch—and she reached out and with her fingertips traced the perfection of Kal's profile.

His wide forehead, the high-bridged nose, lingering to trace the outline of those beautifully carved lips.

The thin clothing pressed between them did nothing to disguise the urgent response of his body and she was seized by a surge of power, of certainty that this was her moment and, leaning into him so that her lips touched his, she whispered, 'Please…'

As her fingers, her lips touched his, took possession of his mouth, Kalil al-Zaki, a man known for his ice-cold self-control, consigned his reputation to oblivion.

His arms were already about her and for a moment he allowed himself to be swept away. To feel instead of think.

Drink deep of the honeyed sweetness of a woman who was clever, funny, heartbreakingly lovely. Everything a man could ever want or desire.

Forget, just for a while, who he was. Why he was here.

Her mouth was like silk, her body eager, desperate even, but it wasn't enough and, lost to all sense as he breathed in the scent of her skin, the hollows of her neck, her shoulders, he slowly peeled away the swimsuit to taste the true rosebuds it concealed.

Her response was eager, as urgent as his own, and yet, even as she offered him everything, he could not let go, forget the lies…

How she'd played the virgin, acted the seductress. Was this just another lie to buy his silence?

She whimpered into his mouth as he broke free, determined to regain control of his senses, yet unable to let go as she melted against him.

'Who are you?' he demanded helplessly. 'Why are you here?' When she didn't answer he leaned back, needing to look her in the face, wanting her to see his. But her eyes were closed, as if by not seeing, she would be deaf to his words. 'What do you want from me?'

'Nothing!' Then, more gently, 'I'm sorry.' And, without looking at him, she slowly disentangled herself and, shivering, clutched her costume to her and said, 'You can g-go fishing now, Kal. I promise I'll g-go and sit by the pool like the well behaved young woman I'm supposed to be.'

Torn between wanting her to behave and wanting her to be very, very bad indeed, he reassembled the shattered pieces of his cast-iron self-control, picked up his shirt and, taking her hands, fed them into the sleeves, buttoning it around her as if she were a child.

'I'm going nowhere until you tell me the truth,' he said. Then, with a muttered oath, 'You're shivering.' She couldn't be cold… 'What can I get you?'

'A proper cup of tea?' She sniffed and he lifted her chin, wiped a tear from beneath her eye.

Shivering, tears… He wanted to shake her, hold her, yell at her, make love to her…

'Tea?' he said, trying to get a grip.

'Made in a mug with a tea bag, milk from a cow and two heaped spoons of sugar.' She managed a rueful smile. 'Stirred, not shaken.'

'I'm glad your sense of humour survived intact,' he said.

'My sense of humour and everything else.' She lifted her

shoulders in a simple up and down shrug. 'I've only come that close to losing my virginity once before, Kal. I'm beginning to think I'm destined to be an old maid and the really bad news is that I'm allergic to cats.'

Better make that two cups of hot, sweet tea, he thought, picking up the phone.

# CHAPTER TEN

'WHO are you?'

Lydia, her hands around the mug of tea he'd rustled up for her, was sitting in the shuttered balcony of her room, bars of sunlight slanting through into a very private space and shimmering off Kal's naked shoulders.

'What are you?'

'Lydia. Lydia Young. I've been a professional lookalike pretty much from the moment that Lady Rose made her first appearance.'

'Lydia.' He repeated her name carefully, as if memorising it. 'How old were you?'

'Fifteen. I'm a few months younger than Rose.' She sipped at the hot tea, shuddering at the sweetness. 'How did you know?' Then, because it was somehow more important, 'When did you know?'

'I think that on some level I always knew you weren't Rose.' He glanced at her. 'I sensed a dual personality. Two people in the same body. And you have an unusual turn of phrase for a young woman with your supposedly sheltered upbringing. Then there was the Marchioness slaving over Sunday lunch. And Mrs Latimer.'

'Year Six French.' She took another sip of tea. 'I knew you'd picked up on that. I hoped I'd covered it.'

'You might have got away with it but once that text arrived

you were in bits. It wasn't difficult to work out that you'd be heading for the beach as soon as you'd got rid of me so, while I waited for you to show up, I took a look at the Internet, hoping to pick up some clue about what the hell was going on.'

'What was the clincher?' she asked. Not a Lady Rose word, but she wasn't pretending any more.

'You made the front page in that cute little hat you were wearing. The caption suggested that after recent concerns about your health you appeared to be full of life. Positively glowing, in fact. Fortunately for you, they put it down to true love.'

She groaned.

'I should have done more with my make-up, but we were sure the veil would be enough. And it was all going so well that I might just have got a bit lippy with the photographers. What an idiot!'

'Calm down. There was nothing in the stories to suggest that you were a fake,' he assured her. 'Just a recent photograph of Rose with Rupert and some salacious speculation about what you'd be doing here.'

'But if you had no trouble spotting the difference—'

'Only because I've become intimately acquainted with your face, your figure,' he said. 'I don't pay a lot of attention to celebrity photographs, but the "people's angel" is hard to miss and I expected someone less vivid. Not quite so…' He seemed lost for an appropriate adjective.

'Lippy?' she offered helpfully.

'I was going to say lively,' he said, his eyes apparently riveted to her mouth. 'But lippy will do. One look at the real thing and I knew you were someone else.' Then, turning abruptly, he said, 'So what's going on? Where is Rose Napier? With Rupert Devenish?'

'Good grief, I hope not.'

'Strike two for Rupert. Lucy isn't a fan either. I take it you've met him?'

'I've seen him with her. He's an old style aristocrat. Her grandfather,' she explained, 'but thirty years younger.'

'Controlling.'

She thought about it for a moment, then nodded. 'Rose and I met by chance one day. I'd been booked for a lookalike gig, a product launch at a swanky hotel. I had no idea Rose was going to be a guest at a lunch there or I'd have turned it down, but as I was leaving we came face to face. It could have been my worst nightmare but she was so sweet. She really is everything they say she is, you know.'

'That's another reason I saw through you.' He reached out, wiped the pad of his thumb across her mouth. 'You're no angel, Lydia Young.'

She took another quick sip of her tea.

'How is it?'

'Just what the doctor ordered. Too hot, too sweet. Perfect, in fact.'

'I'll remember the formula.'

She looked at him. Remember? There was a future?

Realising just how stupid that was, she turned away. Just more shocks, she decided, and concentrated on getting through her story.

'Rose spent a little too long chatting with me for Rupert's liking and when he summoned her to heel she asked me how much I charged. In case she ever wanted an evening off.'

'How much do you charge?' he asked pointedly.

'This one is on the house, Kal. I owe Rose. My father was killed in a car accident when I was ten years old. My mother was badly injured—'

'Your brave, determined mother.'

'She lost the man she loved, the use of her legs, her career in the blink of an eye, Kal.'

'I'm sorry.'

She shook her head. It was a long time since she'd cried for the loss and when he reached out as if to take her hand, offer comfort, she moved it out of reach. Right now, comfort would undo her completely and she was in enough trouble without that.

'Is this what you do? I mean, is it a full-time job?'

'Hardly. Two or three gigs a month at the most. The day job is on the checkout at a supermarket. The manager is very good about me swapping shifts.' She was going to tell him that he wanted her to take a management course. As if that would make any difference... 'The money I earn as Rose's lookalike has made a real difference to my mother's life.'

The electric wheelchair. The hand-operated sewing machine. The car she'd saved up for. And the endless driving lessons before she'd eventually passed her test.

'So, like Rose, you have no other family?'

She shook her head.

'And, like her, no lover? You are a beautiful, vivid woman, Lydia. I find that hard to believe.'

'Yes, well, I live a rather peculiar life. My day job is in a supermarket, where staff and customers alike call me Rose despite the fact that I wear a badge with my real name on it. Where most of them can't quite decide whether I'm fish or fowl. The rest of the time I'm pretending to be someone else.'

'And taking care of your mother. I imagine that takes a chunk out of your time, too. Who is with her while you're here?'

'A friend stays with her sometimes so that I can take a holiday. And I'm not totally pathetic. I do get asked out. Of course I do. But I'm never sure exactly who they think they're with.'

'Someone must have got through. If we... If I... If that was the second time.'

She nodded. 'He said he was a law student. He always came to my checkout at the supermarket. Chatted. Brought me tiny gifts. Wooed me with sweet words and posies, flattery and patience. Endless patience. It was weeks before he asked me out.'

Months before he'd suggested more than a kiss. So long that she'd been burning up with frustration. Ready to go off like a fire-cracker.

'It was the patience that did it,' she said. 'The understanding.

How many men are prepared to put up with the missed dates, always coming second to my mother, the job, the gigs? To wait?'

'A man will wait for what is precious,' Kal said.

'And who could resist that?' Not her. She'd fallen like a ton of bricks. 'It was that flash, bang, wallop love thing that you so distrust, Kal. In this case with good reason because when I say precious, I do mean precious. My worth, it seems, was above rubies.'

She could have made a lot of money selling the story to the newspapers but she'd never told anyone what had happened. Not her mother. Not her friends. Not even the agency that employed her. But, sitting here in this quiet space above a beautiful garden carved out of the desert, nothing but the truth would do. She had lied to Kal, hidden who she was, and if she was to win his trust now, win him over so that she could fulfil her promise to Rose, she had to strip herself bare, tell him everything.

'When he asked me to go away for the weekend I felt like the sun was shining just for me. He made it so special, booked the honeymoon suite in a gorgeous hotel in the Cotswolds. I suppose I should have wondered how a student could afford it, but I was in love. Not thinking at all.'

'So what went wrong?'

'Nothing, fortunately. The "Lady Rose" effect saved me.'

He frowned. Well, why wouldn't he? Unless you'd lived it, how would anyone know?

'An elderly chambermaid—a woman who'd seen just about everything in a long career making beds—thought I was Rose and she waylaid me in the corridor to warn me, told me where to find the hidden cameras.'

She swallowed. Even now the memory of it chilled her.

'When I confronted my "student" he confessed that he was an actor who'd been hired to seduce me by a photographer who intended to make a fortune selling pictures of "Lady Rose" losing her virginity with some good-looking stud. Someone who worked in the hotel was in on it, of course. He even offered me a cut of the proceeds if I'd go ahead with it since, as he so eloquently put it, "I was gagging for it anyway". I declined and since then…' she shrugged '…let's say I've been cautious.'

'And yet you still believe in love?'

'I've seen it, Kal. My parents were in love. They lit up around each other and my mother still has a dreamy look whenever she talks about my dad. I won't settle for less than that.' She looked at him. 'I hope that Rose won't either. That this week away from everyone, being anonymous, will help her decide. Will you let her have that?'

'She's safe?' Kal asked, reserving judgement.

'She's been wrapped in cotton wool all her life. I've loaned her my car and right now she's as safe as any anonymous woman taking a few days to do something as simple as shopping without ending up like the Pied Piper of Hamelin, or appearing on the front page of next day's newspaper eating a hot dog.'

'So what was the panic this morning?'

'I think someone must have said something that panicked her. She's not as used to people commenting on the fact that she looks like Lady Rose as I am.' She used her free hand to make little quotes, put on a quavery voice. '"Has anyone ever told you you look a bit like Lady Rose, dear?"'

Kal smiled, but wondered what it must be like to always be told you look like someone else. Whether she sometimes longed for someone to say that Lady Rose looked like her.

'I'll bet that gets old. How do you cope?'

'It depends. If some old biddy whispers it to me in the supermarket, I whisper back that I really am Lady Rose and I'm doing undercover research into working conditions. Warn her not to tell a soul, that she's spotted me. Then wait to see how long it takes before she points me out to someone.'

'That's really bad.'

'You said it, Kal. I'm no angel.'

And for a moment he thought only about the touch of her

lips beneath his fingers, the taste of them beneath his mouth. Then forced himself to remember that she had deceived him. Put his own mission in jeopardy. If the Emir, the Princess ever discovered the truth...

'Sometimes I do a flustered "good heavens, do you really think so, no one has ever said that before" routine,' she said, distracting him with the whole surprised expression, fluttery hand to chest routine.

'I like that one,' he said, which brought that light-up-the-day smile bubbling to her face.

'My favourite is the one where I put on a slightly puzzled smile...' she did a perfect version of the world famous luminous smile that was about a hundred watts less bright than her natural one '...and say "Only a bit?" and wait for the penny to drop.'

'You're a bit of a clown on the quiet, aren't you, Lydia Young?'

'Quiet?' she repeated.

He'd caught glimpses of this lively woman beneath the Rose mantle, but in full flood she was irresistible. Now that she'd stepped out of the shadows, was wholly herself, he knew that it was the lippy woman desperate to break out of the restraints of being Lady Rose that he desired, liked more and more. Her laughter lit him up, her smile warmed him. Even when he was furious with her he wanted to kiss her, wrap her up in his arms and keep her safe, love her...

'Maybe that wasn't the most appropriate word,' he said quickly. 'Did you never consider a career as an actress?'

'No.'

One minute they were laughing, the next they weren't.

'No more,' she said. 'I can't do this any more, Kal. I shouldn't be here. Rose shouldn't be hiding and I shouldn't be living a pretend life.'

'No.' Then, 'You've stopped shivering.'

'Nothing like tea for shock,' she said.

'I'm sorry if I frightened you.'

'Only for about a millisecond. Then I knew it was you.'

'I was angry,' he said.

Lydia swallowed, nodded. Of course he was angry. He'd been charged with protecting her—protecting Rose—and she had sneaked off the minute his back was turned.

'You had every right,' she said. 'But you stuck around to look out for me, even when you knew I wasn't Rose.'

Long after her momentary fear had been forgotten, she'd still feel his strong, protective arm as he'd held her against him. She recalled the warm scent of his skin.

She wouldn't need a shell or anything else to remember that. Remember him.

'So,' she said, sensing the weight of unspoken words between them and, recalling his earlier tension, she repeated the question she'd asked him then, 'what's your problem, Kal? What aren't you telling me?'

'Not just lovely, not just cool under pressure and a loyal friend, but smart, too,' he said, not looking at her. 'You're right, of course. I have a confession to make.'

'You got me at lovely,' she said. Then, because when a man needed to confess, it was never going to be good news, she summoned up all the flippancy at her command and said, 'Don't tell me. You're married.'

No one would have guessed that, in the time it took him to answer, her heart had skipped a beat. Two. Maybe he was right. She should take up acting.

'No, Lydia, I'm not married.'

'Engaged?' This time the pause was longer, but he shook his head.

'That wasn't totally convincing,' she said.

'I am not in a relationship of any kind.'

Better, but there was something he wasn't telling her. Maybe if she shut up and let him get on with his 'confession' in his own way it would all become clear.

It took another half a dozen heartbeats before he said, 'I want you to understand that Lucy was truly concerned for

Rose. Her grandfather tried to talk her into withdrawing the invitation, said there had been a threat of some kind.'

'A threat? What kind of threat?' she asked, alarmed.

'Lucy was certain there was nothing, that it was just a ploy to keep her under his control, but she had to do something to pacify the Duke so she told him that the Emir's nephew would be in charge of his granddaughter's security.'

'That would be you. And he was happy with that?'

'No, but he couldn't object without offending the Emir.'

'And what about the Emir? Wasn't Lucy afraid of offending her father-in-law?'

'She saved Hanif. She can get away with things that no one else would dare to. Even be my friend. My grandfather is dying, Lydia. He lives only to return to Ramal Hamrah to die in the house where he was born.'

Her hand found his and she squeezed it, knowing how much he loved the old man.

'Lucy knew that Princess Sabirah would want to pay her respects to Rose and she seized the chance to put me where I could make a personal appeal to her, beg her to intercede with her husband.'

'And?'

'That first. Above everything…'

'But, once he has been allowed home, you hope the rest will follow. That you can become a Khatib again. With everything that entails.' His name, his title…

'It is as if I have been cut off from half my life. I have the language, I have property here, can study the culture, the history, but without my family…'

The metaphorical clock struck twelve. Time for the coach to turn back into a pumpkin, for Cinderella to go back to the checkout and check out the alternatives to getting a cat. Maybe a rabbit or a guinea pig, she thought. Or half a dozen white mice. Just in case the fairy godmother ever dropped in again.

'Not just your name, your title, but you want the ultimate prize of an arranged marriage to one of the precious daughters of a powerful Ramal Hamrahn family.'

His silence was all the answer she needed.

'That was why you stopped.' She swallowed. 'Would not make love with me.'

'Honour would not allow it,' he agreed.

Honour. What a rare word, but this man who'd been raised in the west was steeped in the culture that had excluded him.

'Absolutely,' she agreed. The kitchen telegraph would be humming to news of an affair before they disturbed the sheets. Princess Sabirah would suddenly find herself too busy to call and all Kal's hopes and dreams would fly right out of the window. 'Good call.'

Lydia stood up, pushed open one of the shutters, looked out over the garden, needing a little space to recover, put the smile back on.

'I'm glad that we were able to be honest with one another, Kal.'

Honest.

This was honest?

This was honour?

Lydia was pretending to be someone she was not, while he was about to collude with her deception, not just of the world's press but the Emir of Ramal Hamrah.

She turned to him.

'Will you take me to the souk tomorrow? I'd like to buy a gift for my mother.'

The request was simple enough, but that wasn't the question she was asking. They both knew it and when, after the briefest pause, he responded in the affirmative with a slight but formal bow, he was confirming that there would be a tomorrow for 'Lady Rose' at Bab el Sama.

What choice did he have?

He had been prepared to be patient, wait for those precious things he wanted for himself, no matter how long it took. But for his grandfather time was running out, leaving him with no choice but to seize the chance Lucy had given him.

She wasn't sure that honour had much to do with it, but love was there in abundance.

'You should believe in love, Kal,' she said. 'You are living proof of its existence. Your love of your family shines through when you talk of them. You yearn with all your heart for this country, for everything that you have lost here and yet you would risk it all on this chance to bring your grandfather home. That's love at its finest. Unselfish, pure, the real thing.'

'I am asking a great deal of you, Lydia. I would understand if you said you could not go through with it.'

'We both have debts, Kal, and to pay them we need each other.' Then, 'You'll excuse me if I ask you to leave now? I need to change.'

Kal watched her wrap herself in the figurative mantel of Lady Rose Napier. Stand a little taller, inject the crispness back into her voice as she distanced herself from him. And where he had been warmed by her smile, her presence, a touch as she'd reached out without thinking, there was now an icy chill.

'Will you come to the stables in the morning?' he asked.

He saw her neck move as she swallowed, glimpsed a momentary longing for the closeness that would give them as he lifted her to the saddle, fitted her feet in the stirrups, placed her hands just so on the reins.

Then she shook her head just once and said, 'Lady Rose is afraid of horses.'

'And Lydia?'

'It's safer to stick to Rose, don't you think?'

He wasn't thinking. That was the problem. He'd set out on a quest that he'd believed nothing in the world could distract him from. How wrong could one man be?

He leaned forward, kissed her cheek. 'I'll send Yatimah to you.'

\* \* \*

When Yatimah arrived, Lydia was filling the huge sunken bath.

'*Sitti!*' she declared. 'I must do that for you.' Then, 'Bin Zaki says that you are going to the souk tomorrow. I will bring you an *abbayah* to keep the dust from your clothes,' she said as she ladled something into the bath that foamed magically, filling the air with an exotic, spicy fragrance. 'Would you like me to wash your hair?'

'Not tonight. I'm really tired so I'll just take a bath and then go to bed.'

She closed the bathroom door, locked it. Leaned back against it. Lifted her hand to her cheek.

Flash, bang, wallop…

Kal walked along the shore that she had walked, but went much further before sitting on a rock and calling his grandfather in London. He didn't ask how he was feeling. He knew he would be in pain because he refused to slide into the morphine induced coma that would lead to death.

Instead, he described the scene before him. The lights along the far shore, the boats riding on the water, the moon rising, dripping, from the ocean so that he could, in his heart, be here with him.

He called his mother, who'd complained of a cold the last time they'd spoken, listened to her news, her happiness at becoming a grandmother again. She demanded to know when he was going to settle down and add to her joy.

Talked to a brother who was struggling at university. Made a promise to go and see him soon.

This was what Lydia called love, he thought. Joint memories that needed only a word to bubble to the surface. Shared connections, history. To know that you could reach out and there would be a hand waiting.

Without that, how would you ever know how to see beyond the fireworks and make a marriage?

How could you ever know for sure?

He was still holding the phone and he scrolled through his contact list until he found 'Rose'.

'Kal?'

Was that it? When just the sound of her voice made your heart sing?

'Where are you, Kal?'

'On the beach, watching the moon rise. I called my grand-father so that he could share it.'

'And now you're sharing it with me?' she asked, still distant, still 'Rose'.

'I'm making a memory, Lydia.' One that, for the rest of their lives, whenever either of them looked at the rising moon would bring back this moment. 'Go onto your balcony and you will see it rise above the trees.'

He heard her move. A door opening. A tiny breath that was not quite a gasp, not quite a sigh. 'It's there,' she said. 'I can just see the top of it.'

'Be patient…'

Was it when you could sit miles apart watching the same spectacle and words weren't necessary?

'Thank you, Kal,' she said, minutes later when it was high enough to have cleared the trees around Bab el Sama. Her voice softer. Pure Lydia.

'*Afwan ya habibati, hada mussdur sa'adati,*' he replied. Then, when she'd broken the connection, 'It is the source of my pleasure, beloved.'

Lydia stood on the terrace at dawn, sipping the orange juice that Dena had brought her, staying to watch Kal ride along the beach.

'He is faster this morning,' Dena said enigmatically. 'The demons must be getting closer.'

'Yes,' she replied without thinking. 'They are.'

She'd scarcely slept—at this rate she would soon look

exactly like Rose—and had watched the sky grow light, barely able to stop herself from going to the stables, just to be near him.

'Come, *sitti,* I will prepare you.'

Two hours later, resolved to keep her distance and wearing a feather-light black silk wrap, she and Kal crossed the creek to visit the souk.

It started well enough. They'd kept a clear foot between them and the conversation safely on topics such as the weather, Arabic vocabulary, followed by a whole lot of incoherent babbling as she'd seen the amazing array of colourful spices that came in dustbin-sized containers instead of tiny little glass jars.

Neither of them had mentioned the full moon they'd watched rising from the far ends of Bab el Sama. Apart and yet more intensely together than if they had been in each other's arms.

'Would you like the full tour?' he asked, 'or shall we go straight for the good stuff?'

She gave him a 'Lady Rose' look and said, 'The full tour. I want to see everything.'

Maybe that was the wrong answer. The area where the blacksmiths worked was noisy, hot and sparks flew everywhere. There were tinsmiths hammering away too and carpenters repairing furniture.

Once they turned into an area where tailors were waiting to run her up a dress in an hour or two things improved. There were tiny shops containing all kinds of strange and wonderful foods that weren't on the shelves of the supermarket that was her second home. She tasted Turkish delight flavoured with cardamom, a glass of tea from a man wandering about with an urn, little sticky cakes from a stall.

It was a different world and she sucked up every experience, her guard dropping long before they reached the stalls piled high with gorgeous silks.

Once there, she realised that she was not alone in wearing western clothes beneath the *abbayyeh*. There were plenty of woman who, when they leaned forward to look at the goods on display, revealed business suits, trousers, simple dresses beneath them. And although her pale hair and blue eyes made her an obvious foreigner, no one took much notice.

'They're used to Lucy and her friends,' Kal said. 'And another cousin, Zahir, is married to an English woman, too. A redhead in his case.'

'I read about it,' she said. 'It caused quite a sensation but I had no idea he was your cousin. Do you know him?'

'Our paths have crossed,' he said. 'We're in the same business.' He shrugged. 'My planes carry freight. His carry passengers.'

'Air freight? When you said you'd hadn't quite broken the habit of acquiring planes, you weren't joking, were you?'

'I ran out of room, so I had to keep some of them in the air,' he said. Joking, obviously. He had to be joking. 'Have you decided what you want?' he asked.

'It's impossible, but I've narrowed it down to three,' she said.

'I thought you were looking at this one?' He lifted the edge of a rich, heavy cream silk that would be perfect for a wedding dress.

'It's lovely,' she said, 'but I have no use for it.'

'Why do you have to have a use for something?' With a gesture that took in all four fabrics, he spoke briefly to the stall-holder. Moved on.

'Kal,' she protested. 'I haven't paid. I haven't told him how much I want. And what about my parcels?'

'He'll deliver them. And Dena will settle with him. Unless you want to haggle?'

Giving it up as a lost cause, she said, 'No, thanks. I'd rather hear more about this air freight business of yours. Does it have a name?'

'Kalzak Air Services.'

'Kalzak? That's your company?' Even she'd heard of them. Everybody had heard of them. 'I…um…hadn't made the connection. It's not exactly a hobby, then?'

'No,' he admitted. 'It's not a hobby. But I wasn't interested in the family business.'

She frowned. He hadn't mentioned a family business but there must be one or how else had they supported all those wives, children?

'Exiled playboy?' he prompted.

'I'm sorry—'

He stopped her fumbling apology with a touch to the elbow. 'It's okay. My grandfather lost his throne, but his father made a generous financial settlement—probably out of guilt.'

'And his brother didn't take that away?'

'He couldn't have, even if he'd wanted to, but I imagine he thought he was less dangerous playing with his racehorses and women than taking to the hills and fermenting more trouble.'

'You said he was the clever one.'

She thought that Kal was a lot more like his great-uncle, with his work ethic and philanthropy, than the grandfather he adored.

'Well, you and your cousin have something in common. Isn't that a starting place?'

'I help Lucy out when she needs to move disaster relief supplies. Zahir al-Khatib suggested I was taking advantage of her and offered to carry anything she needed so that she wouldn't have to turn to me for help.'

'Oh…'

And then, just when she was feeling desperately sorry for him, he gave her one of those slow smiles calculated to send her hormones into a dizzy spin.

'She probably shouldn't have told him that I had more aircraft, fewer family commitments. That I could afford to bear the cost more easily. His airline is very new,' he explained. 'But she wanted him to understand that my participation wasn't a matter for discussion.'

'Honestly,' she declared, 'I was just about to open up my heart and bleed for you.'

'I know.' And he touched the spot just by her mouth where she had pointed out his own giveaway muscle. 'You probably shouldn't ever play poker unless you're wearing a full face mask, Lydia,' he said softly. Then, as if nothing had happened, 'Gold next, I think.'

She followed him on rubbery legs to the glittering gold souk where the metal shone out of tiny shop windows and the air itself seemed to take on a golden glow.

It was a stunning spectacle and she could have spent hours there, but she quickly chose a pair of earrings, a waterfall of gold and seed pearls for her mother—who wore her hair up and adored dangly earrings—and a brooch set with turquoise for Jennie for looking after her.

'You will not choose something for yourself?'

He lifted the heavy rose pendant she was wearing at her throat. 'I imagine you'll have to give this back?'

'You imagine right.' But she could read him too, and she shook her head. 'Don't!' Then, 'Please, don't even think it…' she said, and walked quickly away in the direction of the harbour and the launch that had brought them across the creek, knowing that he had no choice but follow.

But later that afternoon four bolts of cloth were delivered to her room. And when she asked about paying for them Dena simply shrugged and suggest that she ask 'bin Zaki.'

Lydia didn't know much about the protocol in these things, but she was fairly certain that a man on the lookout for a bride was not supposed to buy another woman anything, let alone something as personal as cloth she would wear next to her skin.

Easy to see, in retrospect, that the spark that flared between them had been lit in the first moment they had set eyes on one another and for a moment it had burned so intense that, even while he was single-mindedly focused on his future, he had still come close to losing control.

There could be nothing 'little' between them and she was holding herself together with nothing but willpower.

# CHAPTER ELEVEN

LYDIA wanted this over. Was desperate for Princess Sabirah to pay her call and the week to be over so that she could just stop pretending and go home.

Stop pretending to be Rose. Stop pretending that she felt nothing for Kalil. Not that that worked. He'd only had to call in the darkness. She only had to hear his voice. If she hadn't cared she would have hung up, not stood there with her phone pressed to her ear, imagining she could hear him breathe while that huge moon rose above them.

Why had he done that?

He was the one who'd stepped back from the brink, broken the most intense, the most intimate connection there could ever be between a man and a woman even when it was obvious he'd wanted her as much as she'd wanted him.

Trapped, like her, committed to a course from which there was no escape but unable to stop himself from touching her. Calling her. Making love to her with words.

Breaking her heart.

She had taken lunch alone, keeping her nose firmly in a book until the words all ran together in a smeary blur, swam fifty lengths of the pool just to stop herself from thinking about him.

Except that when she emerged, slightly dizzy with the effort, he was waiting to wrap a towel around her.

'You shouldn't be here,' she said.

'I am your bodyguard. It is my duty.'

'I'm not in any danger.'

Only from falling in love with a man who didn't believe in love. Who thought marriage was no more than a convenient contract arranged by two families for their advantage. Maybe the girls did have some say, but the pressure had to be intense to make a 'good' marriage. Scarcely any different from the way that medieval barons gave their daughters to men whose land marched with theirs, or who could bring them closer to the King.

'Please…' She grabbed the towel and ran from the poolside to her room. Sat with it pressed to her face.

'Be strong, Lydie. You have to be strong…'

But, no matter how she ignored him, Kal's presence permeated the house.

Everywhere she went, she was sure he'd been there a second before. She couldn't escape the woody scent that clung to him, the swish of freshly laundered robes, the gentle flapping sound of leather thongs against marble floors.

The thrumming beat of hooves against sand.

It was all in her head, she knew, but she retreated to her room, allowing Yatimah to pamper her with facials, massage the tension out of her shoulders, paint more ornate patterns on her hands and feet with henna.

She caught sight of them as she reached for the phone, hoped they would wear off before she went back to work or they'd cause a few comments from the regulars as she swished their weekly shop over the scanner.

She checked the caller ID and, when she saw it was Kal, considered not answering. But then he'd come looking for her.

She took a deep breath, composed herself.

'Kal?' she queried, ice-cool.

'Just checking. I haven't seen you all day. Are you hiding from me?'

*Reckless, bold, dangerous Bagheera, whose skin shimmered like watered silk, whose mouth tasted like wild honey—only a fool wouldn't hide.*

'Just putting my feet up, taking it easy while I plan my future,' she said.

'Oh? What did you have in mind?'

'Well,' she said, her fingers lingering on the bolt of cream silk on the table beside her, 'now I'm giving up the lookalike business I thought I might set myself up in the rag trade,' she said. 'Costing is tricky, though. I need to know how much to budget for material.'

'Oh, I see. This is about the silk…'

'I can't wear it all myself,' she pointed out. Not unless she made a wedding dress with a thirty foot train. 'I need to know how much it cost.'

'You must ask Dena. She dealt with the merchant.'

'She told me to ask you.'

'Then it's a mystery,' he said with an infuriating hint of laughter in his voice that undid all her good intentions, all her cool.

'Kal!' she exploded. 'I just wanted a few metres for a suit or dress. I can't take all that home with me.'

'No problem.' Now he was enjoying himself. 'I'll deliver.'

'Deliver them to your bride,' she snapped. 'Yatimah was telling me that's what a groom is supposed to do. Send jewels, cloth, carpets, the biggest flat screen television you can afford.'

'Yatimah has altogether too much to say for herself,' he snapped back and she rejoiced in having rattled him out of his teasing. He had no right to tease her. No right to call her and make her want him… For a moment neither of them spoke and the only sound was of raised breathing. Then, after a moment, his voice expressionless, his manner formal, Kal said, 'Lucy phoned to check up on how well I've been looking after you, *sitti*.'

'Tell her what you like,' Lydia replied, not even trying for cool. 'I won't tell tales. And cut out the *sitti*.' It was one thing having Dena or Yatimah calling her 'lady', quite another from Kal.

'I can't tempt you to come on a picnic?'

Oh, the man knew how to tempt.

She refused without having to think twice. Well, maybe twice, but she knew the attraction between them was too great to risk another close encounter. And that even while he was paying lip service to honour, his frustrated libido was refusing to quit.

'Sorry, Kal, but I'm planning a walk on the beach this afternoon and, unlike you, I'm happy with my own company,' she said, knowing how much that would infuriate him. But she was angry with him for putting her through this, with herself for aching for something so far out of reach. For bringing tears stinging to her eyes. 'But you're welcome to stand and watch if you like. Just remember how handy I am with a shell.'

She didn't wait for him to command her not to do it, but hung up. Then had to hold herself together. Physically wrap her arms around herself, holding her breath, just to stop herself from falling apart.

Kal took himself to the stables in the foulest, blackest mood.

He was behaving like a man who didn't know his own mind. Who had lost control of his senses.

It wasn't true. When he could have taken Lydia, he had known it was wrong. That, without commitment, honour, such an act was beneath him, could only hurt her.

He'd hurt her anyway.

She could hide nothing from him and he'd seen her eyes in the moment she had realised why he had refused the greatest gift a woman could bestow on any man. Had seen her pain in the way she'd moved as she'd taken herself away from him in the souk, when all he'd wanted to do was shower her with gold, pearls. Put diamonds in her ears, on every one of the fingers he had taken to his lips. When, seeing that in his face, she had begged him not even to think it.

He was furious because, even as he weakened, unable to stay

away, she grew stronger, keeping him at arm's length when he needed them around her.

A nagging, desperate need that came from somewhere deep inside, from a place he hadn't, until that moment, known existed. All he knew was that he was ready to consign common sense, five years of patient planning along with everything he had learned about the fleeting nature of 'love' from his grandfather, his father, to the deep blue sea.

And still she had turned him down. Not because she didn't want to go. He was attuned to every nuance in her voice, every hesitation and he'd heard the unspoken longing in a whisper of a sigh before she had said no to his picnic.

But, even when he was losing control, she was strong enough to save him from himself.

Lydia Young might not be a princess, but she had all the attributes of one. Courage, dignity that would become a queen. A spirit that was all her own. He wanted her with a desperation that was driving every other thought from his head.

At home he would have taken up the small biplane he used for stunting, shaken off his mood in a series of barrel rolls, loops. Here, the closest he could get to a release in the rush of power was on one of Hanif's fine stallions but, as he tightened the girth, the horse skipped edgily away from him, sensing his frustration.

But it wasn't simply his out of control libido, the sense of being too big for his skin. This was a need that went much deeper, challenging everything he believed in.

He'd spent the last five years planning the perfect life but Lydia was forcing him to face the fact that life wasn't something that you could plan. It happened. Some of it good, some of it bad, none of it 'safe'.

He had arrogantly assumed that his grandfather, his father had wasted their lives but, while their families were scarcely conventional, their quivers were full of the children of their youth and they were, he realised with a shock, happy men.

That, wherever his grandfather died, he would be surrounded by his children, grandchildren, people who loved him.

He lay his hand on the neck of the horse, gentling him with soft words, even while he yearned for the sound of Lydia's voice. The sweet scent that clung to her, as if she had been brushing her hands over jasmine. The touch of her hands against his skin.

Wanted to see her face, her eyes lighting up, her mouth softening, her hands describing what her lips were saying. Her quickness with a tender touch to show that she understood. Her laugh. The swiftness with which she melted to his kisses.

While he kept the world at bay, carefully avoiding the risk, the pain that was an inevitable part of what Lydia called 'love', she held nothing back.

She had answered every question he had asked of her with not just her body, but her heart and her soul and he wanted to shower her with gifts, buy her every bolt of cloth in the market, heap up gold, pearls, gems in a dower that she could not ignore.

Except, of course, she could and would. She had told him so. Her price was above rubies. Only his heart, freely given in an avowal of love, without negotiations, conditions, guarantees would win her acceptance.

She would not settle for less and neither, he knew now, would he. Because the nearest a man could come to perfection was to take every single moment and live it to the full. With love. And she was right. He was not a stranger to the emotion. Love for his family was part of who he was.

But this was new. This love for a woman who, from the first moment he had set eyes on her, had made the lights shine more brightly.

He'd lost the perfect moment, had hurt her. Now, to show her how he felt, he had to give her not just his heart but his world. Everything that made him who he was. And there was only one way he could do that, could win her trust.

The horse snorted impatiently, eager to be off, but he left the groom circling the yard as he made the calls that would change his life.

Lydia stepped onto the beach, kicking off her sandals. It was cooler today and she was wearing cotton trousers, a white shirt, a cashmere sweater knotted at her waist.

There were clouds gathering offshore and the wind coming off the sea was sharper, whipping up little white horses on the creek and, as she strode along the beach, hanging onto her temper by a thread, she glowered at the photographer's launch, bobbing on the waves, hoping that he was seasick.

She doubted that. There hadn't been pictures in the papers for a day or two. A sighting of Rupert Devenish at a business meeting in the States had downgraded interest in Bab el Sama and he would have packed up his telephoto lenses and gone in search of more lucrative prey.

It hadn't been a great week for anyone, she thought, her hand tightening around the note from Princess Sabirah's secretary that Dena had delivered to her as she'd left for her walk.

It was brief and to the point, informing her, regretfully, that the Princess had a cold and was unable to travel this week. Wishing her a pleasant stay and the Princess's sincere hope that they would meet soon in London.

Somewhere where there was no chance that Kal al-Zaki would pop out of the woodwork, presumably.

That the illness was diplomatic, she had no doubt, and she let out a very unladylike roar of outrage that all Kal's hopes and dreams had been crushed without even a chance to put in a plea for his grandfather.

What on earth was the matter with these people? It had all happened fifty years ago, for heaven's sake.

'Get over it!' she shouted to the sky, the seabirds whirling overhead.

He had to know. She would have to tell him and the sooner the better. Maybe there was still something he could do. She could do…

If she really had been Rose, she could have gone to Rumaillah by herself, taken some flowers to the 'sick' Princess. On her own, she would have been admitted. Could have pleaded for him.

She stopped, stood for a moment staring at the phone in her hand as she realised something else. That with his mission dead he would turn to her for comfort, would be free to love her…

She stopped the thought dead, ashamed even to have given it room in her head, and quickly scrolled down the contact list and hit 'dial'. Unexpectedly, it went straight to voicemail…

'Kal,' she began uncertainly, hating to be the bearer of such bad news. Then, as she hesitated, above the buffeting of the wind she heard another sound. The pounding of hooves. She swung round and saw him riding towards her astride a huge black horse, robes flying behind him, hand outstretched. Before she could think, move, there was a jolt as he swooped low, caught her round the waist, lifted her to his saddle.

It was the dream, she thought crazily as she clung to him, her face pressed against his pounding heart.

She'd reached out to him as she'd watched him from above, wanting to be lifted to the stars.

There were no stars and she knew that at any moment he would slow down, berate her for taking unnecessary risks.

But he didn't stop, didn't slow down until Bab el Sama was far below them, the horse rearing as he brought it to a halt, turned, slid to the ground with her.

'Did your English heart beat to be swept onto my horse, *ya habibati?*' He smiled as he curved his hand around her face. 'Did you feel mine, beloved?' He took her hand and placed it against his chest. 'Feel it now. It beats for you, Lydia Young.'

Beloved…

He had called her his beloved and as his lips came down on hers she was lost.

* * *

'This is kidnapping,' she said when he carried her to a waiting four-by-four. 'Where are you taking me?'

'You will see,' he said as he fastened the seat belt and climbed in beside her. 'Then I will ask you if you wish me to take you back.'

'But what about...?'

He silenced her protest with a kiss.

'The groom will take him back,' he said and she realised that this had not been a spur of the moment escapade but was a carefully arranged assault on her defences by a man who when he offered a treat refused to take no for an answer. No doubt there would be a picnic waiting for her at the side of the river, or some archaeological treasure.

But when he stopped there was nothing but a distant view.

'There,' he said. 'Do you see it?'

She could see something shimmering through the dust haze like a mirage. A tower, a shimmer of green above high walls, and she knew without doubt that she was looking at Umm al Sama.

'I see it,' she said. Then, turning to him, 'I see you, Kalil bin Zaki.'

'Will you go there with me?'

He had brought her to the place where his grandfather had been born. The place he called home. Not home as in the place where he lived, like the apartments in Rumaillah, London, New York, but the home of his heart. The place that an exile, generations on, still carried deep in the memory, in his soul.

That he would keep for a woman who meant more than a brief affair. This was the home he had been preparing not just for the return of his grandfather, but for the bride he would one day bring here and, even though he knew who she was, Lydia Young, he was offering it to her.

Words for a moment failed her, then a phrase came into her head, something from long ago Sunday School...

*'Whither thou goest, I will go; and where thou lodgest, I will lodge…'*

Kal knew this was a perfect moment. He had offered the woman he loved all that he was and she had replied with words that touched his soul and as he reached for her, embraced her, sealed their future with a kiss, he knew he owned the world.

Kal led her through Umm al Sama by the hand, through gardens that had run wild, but were being tamed. Beside pools that had been cleaned and reflected the blue of a sky that had magically cleared above them. Through arched colonnades decorated with cool blue and green tiles.

Showed her a wind tower that funnelled the air down to a deep cooling pool below ground. Buildings that had been beautiful once and would be beautiful again when he had finished restoring them.

One building, smaller than the rest, was finished. Kal watched her from the doorway as she walked around an exquisite sitting room touching fine tables, running a finger over the smooth curves of fine porcelain.

'This is so beautiful, Kal. So special.' She looked at him. 'What was this?'

Kal had not touched Lydia since they'd arrived at Umm al Sama. Outside, in the garden, where they might be seen, he'd kept a discreet distance between them. Showing her respect. He had not brought her here to make love to her, but to give her his heart. To give her this.

'My great-grandfather's wife lived here before they moved to the new palace at Rumaillah.'

'Leaving it to the heir apparent?'

'No one has lived here since my grandfather was banished. If you go upstairs, there should be something to eat on the balcony.'

'All this and food too?'

'I invited you on a picnic,' he reminded her, leading the way to a wide covered balcony with carved shade screens that ran the length of the building.

She stared for a moment at the distant view of the mountains, then pushed open a door to reveal the private apartment of a princess.

The polished floor was covered with rare carpets, the walls hung with vivid gauzy silk, as was the great bed at its heart.

Lydia looked back at him. 'Are you expecting Scheherazade?'

'Only you. Come, *ya habibati*,' he said, extending his hand to her. 'You must be hungry.'

'I'm starving, Kal.' As she raised her hand to meet his, she came into his arms, lifted her lips to his. 'Feed me.'

As she breathed the words into his mouth he shattered. The man who had been Kalil al-Zaki no longer existed. As he shed his clothes, fed Lydia Young, the wife of his heart, with his touch, his mouth, his body, she rebuilt him with her surprise, her delight, tiny cries of pleasure at each new intimacy and finally with her tears as they learned from each other and finally became one.


'I have to go back to Bab el Sama, Kal,' she protested the following morning as she lay in bed while he fed her pomegranate seeds and dates for breakfast. 'I have no clothes here.'

He kissed her shoulder. 'Why do you need clothes?'

'Because otherwise I can't leave this room.'

He nudged the edge of the sheet, taking the kiss lower. 'I repeat, why do you need clothes, *ya rohi, ya hahati?*'

He'd showered her with words she did not understand as he'd made love to her, but she refused to be distracted.

'Dena will be concerned.'

'Dena knows that you are with your bodyguard. Am I not guarding your body?' And his smile, his touch, made everything else go away.

Thoroughly and completely distracted, it was gone noon

when she stirred again. She was alone in the great bed they'd shared and, wrapping the sheet around her, she went to the balcony, expecting to find him there waiting for her to wake.

The balcony was deserted but her clothes, freshly laundered, were waiting for her on a dresser with a note from Kal.

*Ask for whatever you want. Umm al Sama is yours. I will back soon.*

She held it to her breast, smiling. Obviously he'd gone to fetch her clothes, explain their absence, and she bathed, washed her hair, dressed. The note from the princess's secretary, forgotten in the wild excitement of her abduction, of Umm al Sama, of Kal, was at the bottom of the pile. That had been ironed, too.

She should have told him about that. As she put on Rose's watch she wondered what time he'd left. How long it would be before he returned.

Maybe he'd rung. She checked her messages but there was nothing. Tried his number but it went straight to voicemail but this wasn't news she could dump on him that way. And leaving a *When will you be back?* message seemed so needy…

A servant brought her food. She picked at it. Took a walk in the garden.

Checked her phone again. With nothing to read, no one to talk to, she switched to the Net and caught the urgent flash of a breaking news story and her blood ran cold.

*Lady Rose kidnapped…*

Rose…

But it wasn't Rose.

Of course it wasn't. It was her in the picture.

Make that a whole series of pictures.

Alone on the beach. Kal riding her down. Lifting her to his saddle. Disappearing into the distance.

The photographer hadn't gone anywhere, she realised. Or had he been tipped off because he'd had all the time in the world to get the whole story in pictures...?

No question by whom.

There was only one person at Bab al Sama who wanted to be visible.

Well, two. She had wanted to be visible and maybe she'd given Kal the idea. Because when he'd realised that the princess wasn't coming—Dena had no doubt had her own note from the palace and would certainly have told him—he must have been desperate.

Not for himself. Whatever happened, he'd thrown away his own hopes and dreams the minute he'd picked her up from the beach. The family name, the title, the bride. Five years of quiet diplomacy, of being invisible.

He'd done this solely out of love for his grandfather.

For love, she reminded herself as she stared at the pictures for one last moment.

One thing was certain—with the world's press on the case, he was no longer invisible. The Emir could no longer pretend he did not exist. On the contrary, he had probably sent his guard to arrest him, lock him up. That would explain his lengthy absence. Why his phone was switched off.

And only she could save him.

She resisted the temptation to leave him to cool his heels for a night in the cells and went to find someone to take her to Rumaillah.

All he'd planned was a photo opportunity followed by a picnic. She was the one who'd got completely the wrong end of the stick, responding to his polite invitation to visit his family home with a declaration of eternity. Led all the way with her desperate *'I'm starving...feed me'*. What on earth was a man to do faced with that? Say no, thanks—again?

Once she was on her way—and had stopped blushing long enough to think straight—she called Rose. She couldn't have picked up the story yet, or she'd have been on the phone herself. She growled with frustration as her call went straight to voice-mail and she left a reassuring message.

Then she called her mother, not because she'd be worried, but because she really, really needed to hear her voice.

Kal left his beautiful Lydia sleeping. He could have asked for her things to be sent to Umm al Sama, but he wanted to visit the souk.

While she had clearly understood the significance of his taking her to Umm al Sama, that no one but his bride would ever sleep in that bed, he wanted to buy her at least one of the diamonds that he would shower on her.

He left Yatimah to pack their bags while he crossed the creek in search of a perfect solitaire. A stone that would say the things that words could never say. A pledge. A promise of forever.

Then he called his grandfather to tell him that he must not be in such a hurry to die. That, if he was patient, he would see not only a wedding at Umm al Sama but a great-grandson born there, too.

It was after lunch before he arrived home to be told that the *sitti* had insisted on being taken to Rumaillah. To the palace.

Rumaillah...

Had there been a call? A summons from the Princess? No. She would not have made a formal visit wearing a pair of cotton trousers and a shirt. This was something else. He took the stairs two at a time as he raced to the room where they had spent the night in blissful discovery of each other, certain that she must have left a message.

There was nothing.

Only the message he had left for her.

And a note from the palace with Princess Sabirah's regrets...

Dena had told him that she'd been unwell; it was why she

hadn't come earlier. This must have been in Lydia's pocket when he'd taken her from the beach. It couldn't have anything to do with her racing off to Rumaillah.

Unless…

He flipped to the Net, saw the breaking news story. And swore long and inventively in several languages. He'd had the photographer warned off but he'd either come back or this was another one. It made no difference.

He knew exactly what Lydia must be thinking.

She'd assume that he'd known that the Princess was not coming and that he had used her to force the Emir to notice him.

That she'd trusted him with all that she was, given him her most precious gift, and he had betrayed her.

Lydia stood at the door to the *majlis*. She'd borrowed an *abbayeh* from one of the women at Umm al Sama but she was the only woman in the group of people who had arrived to petition the Emir. She was aware of a rumbling of disapproval, a certain amount of jostling, but she stood tall, refused to turn tail and run, and waited her turn.

The room was vast. At one end the Emir sat with his advisors. Along each wall men, drinking coffee from tiny cups, sat on rows of sofas.

As she kicked off her sandals, stepped forward, the *abbayeh* caught—or maybe someone was standing on it—and slipped from her hair and every sound died away.

The Emir rose, extended a hand in welcome and said, 'Lady Rose. We were concerned for your safety. Please…'

He gestured her forward.

She walked the length of the room. Bowed. Said, 'Thank you, Excellency, but as you see I am safe and well. If you have seized Kalil al-Zaki, have him locked in your cells, I must ask you to release him.'

There was a buzz, silenced by a look from the Emir.

'Who is Kalil al-Zaki?' he asked.

She gasped, snapped, 'Who is he? I don't believe you people! It's been fifty years since his grandfather was exiled. Was stripped of everything he cared about. Your nephew has an apartment in this city, yet you treat him as if he did not exist.'

Now there was silence. Pin drop silence, but she was too angry to care that she was flouting royal protocol. Even an Emir needed to hear the truth once in a while.

'Kalil al-Zaki is a man of honour, a man who cares for his family, who has built up an international business that would grace any nation. He wants nothing from you but to bring his grandfather home to die. You would grant that to a dog!' Then, in the ringing silence that followed this outburst, 'And, by the way, my name is Lydia Young. Lady Rose has taken a holiday in a place where she won't be photographed twenty-four hours a day!'

Then, because there was nothing left for her, she sank to her knees before him.

'The son of your great-grandfather is dying, Excellency. Will you not let him come home?'

Kal was too late to stop her. He was blocked at the doorway by the Emiri guard, forced to watch as she berated the Emir.

But, in the deathly silence that followed her appeal for mercy, even they were too stunned to stop him and he pushed the man aside, lifted her to her feet, then touched his head, his heart and bowed to her.

'*Ya malekat galbi, ya rohi, ya hahati.* You are beautiful, my soul, my life. *Ahebbak, ya tao'am rohi.* The owner of my heart. *Amoot feeki.* There is no life without you.' Then, 'I did not know, Lydia. Please believe me, I did not use you. I did not know.'

She would have spoken, but the Emir stepped forward. 'I have listened to your appeal, Lydia Young.'

That she was dismissed, neither of them were in any doubt, but as he turned to leave with her, caring only that she should believe him, the Emir said, 'I have not heard from you, Kalil al-Zaki.'

She touched his hand, said, 'Stay.'

'No…'

'For heaven's sake, Kal. This is what you wanted. Your chance. Don't blow it now.'

Then she turned and walked away.

Lydia had been taken to the Princess's quarters. She'd been fed and given a change of clothes and then, having asked to be allowed to go straight home, the British Consul had been summoned to provide her with temporary papers since her passport was with her belongings and only Kal knew were they were.

She arrived home to a dozen messages from newspapers wanting her story and one from a famous publicist who warned her to sign nothing until she'd talked to him. And reporters knee-deep on the footpath outside her mother's flat.

Her mother didn't say a word. Just hugged her.

Numb until then, she finally broke down and cried.

Rose called to make sure she was really all right. To apologise for the publicity. To thank her.

'You've changed my life, Lydia. Words cannot express my gratitude. You should sell your story, make a mint.'

'There is no story, Rose.' Then, 'Is there any chance of getting my car back soon? I'm due back at work the day after tomorrow.'

'That's a bit of a bad news, good news story, I'm afraid. The bad news is that I had a little bit of an accident,' she confessed.

'Oh.' The car had been her pride and joy. It had taken her forever to save up for it… 'Is it in the garage?'

'Er…a little bit more of an accident than that,' she admitted. 'It's nothing but a cube of metal in a scrapyard, but the good news is that George has arranged a replacement for you. A rather jolly red Beetle. I'll make sure it's delivered tomorrow.'

'Thank you. And Rose. Congratulations. I hope you will be really happy.'

'I'll send you and your mother an invitation to the wedding.'

There was nothing from Kal and, since she didn't want to

hear from the reporters, the newspapers or the publicist, she unplugged the phone and turned off her mobile.

She sent an email to the lookalike agency, informing them that she would no longer be available and asking them to take her off their books.

Deleted dozens from newsmen offering interviews, and weirdos who just wanted to be weird.

She didn't open the door to the manager of the local garage who came to deliver a brand-new red VW Beetle, which she knew cost about three times what she'd paid for her car, until he put a note through the door explaining who he was.

There was no missing the black and gold livery of the Kalzak Air Services courier who pulled up outside and delivered her luggage. All those lovely clothes, the cosmetics, the scent, the four bolts of silk.

She gave her mother and Jennie their gifts.

And then, in the privacy of her room, she cried again all over the cream silk.


The Emir had given Kal a hard time. Made him wait while he consulted his brothers, his sons, his nephews. Hanif had supported him and so, unexpectedly, had Zahir and all the time he had been berating himself for letting Lydia walk away. Fly away.

She had thought he was in trouble and had come to help. Had begged for him.

Only her 'stay' had kept him here while members of a family he did not know video-conferenced from all over the world, deciding the fate of his grandfather, eventually deciding that compassion required that he should be allowed to return to Umm al Sama. And that, after his death, his family could use the name Khatib.

Kal told the Emir that he would bring his grandfather home but under those terms they could keep their name. He didn't want it. Lydia deserved better from him than acceptance of such a mealy-mouthed offer.

And the Emir smiled. 'I remember him. You are just like him.'

'You honour me, Excellency.'

At which point His Excellency had thrown up his hands and said, 'Let the old man have his name and his title.'

'Will you permit Dena to return to London with me to fetch him, travel back with him and his nurses?'

'If she is agreeable.' Then, with heavy irony, 'Is there anything else you want, Kalil bin Zaki al-Khatib? One of my granddaughters as a bride, perhaps, now that you are a sheikh?'

'I am very conscious of the honour you bestow, Excellency,' he replied, 'but, like my grandfather, I have chosen my own bride. You have had the honour of meeting her.'

And this time the Emir laughed appreciatively.

'She is all fire, that one. You will have your hands full.' He did not appear to believe that this was a bad thing.


Since there was no other way to get rid of them, Lydia finally faced the newsmen, standing on the pavement outside her home giving an impromptu press conference, answering their questions.

'Who was the horseman?'

'A bodyguard rescuing me from intrusive photographers.'

Laughter.

'Lady Rose has cut her hair. Will you do that?'

'No.'

'When did you meet?'

'Will you be seeing her?'

'Have you met her fiancé?'

No. No. No.

She kept a smile pinned to her face, didn't lose her temper, even at the most intrusive questions, and eventually they ran out of things to ask.

And since she wasn't Lady Rose, it didn't take long for the madness to die down. One moment the pavement in front of their flat had been mobbed, the next there was no one.

The agency was still pleading with her to reconsider her

decision. They'd been inundated with requests for appearances since Rose had announced her engagement. But the publicist, who'd been so keen to negotiate a contract for her to 'write' the story of her career as Rose's lookalike—with the titillating promise to reveal who had really swept her away on that black stallion and what had happened afterwards—finally accepted that she meant it when she said 'no'.

With the excitement of Rose's engagement to occupy the gossip pages, she quickly became old news.

The story about the exiled Sheikh who had been pardoned by the Emir and allowed to return home to die probably wouldn't have made the news at all, except that Ramal Hamrah was where that very odd incident had taken place, when everyone thought Lady Rose had been kidnapped.

She had heard nothing from Kalil.

No doubt he had his hands full taking care of his grandfather, transferring him to Umm al Sama. Getting to know a whole new family.

She winced as *White Christmas* began to play for the fiftieth time that week on the seasonal tape. Turned to smile at yet another harassed mother doing her Christmas shop. Reached for yet another turkey.

Kal quietly joined the checkout queue.

All his duties done, he had come straight from the airport to find Lydia. Had gone to her home. He'd met her mother and, with her blessing, he had come to claim his love publicly, in her real world. Wanted her to know that there was no misunderstanding between them. That he knew who she was. That it was not some icon he had fallen in love with but Lydia Young.

Not the aristocrat in the designer suit, but the ordinary girl on the supermarket checkout wearing an overall and a ridiculous hat.

She looked exhausted. There were dark shadows beneath her eyes, her cheeks were hollow and had lost their glow, but the smile never faltered.

She greeted regular customers as friends. Asked what they were doing for the holiday and, as she listened with every appearance of interest, they lost a little of their tension as she swiftly dealt with their purchases. He watched her pack the shopping for one old lady whose hands were crippled with arthritis, helped her count out the money.

He made an instinctive move forward to help as she heaved a heavy bag of potatoes over the scanner, got a glare from the woman in front who was fiddling with a mobile phone. She was trying to take a picture of Lydia, he realised, and he leaned forward and said very quietly, 'Don't do that.'

About to tell him to mind his own business, she thought better of it and, muttering something about forgetting something, melted away.

Next in line was a woman with a toddler and a small baby who was grizzling with exhaustion.

Lydia whizzed the goods through, packed the bags, then took the baby, put it to her shoulder as the woman searched helplessly for her wallet. Reassuring the woman, patting the baby. The baby fell asleep, the wallet was found.

'Can I take you home with me?' the woman asked as she retrieved her baby.

He'd seen her dressed in designer clothes, every inch the Lady with a capital L.

He'd seen her sweetness with Yatimah, her eyes hot with passion, soft with desire. Seen her berate the Emir in a room filled with hostile men. Seen her on her knees begging for him...

Beauty was a lot more than skin-deep and with each revelation he'd fallen deeper in love with Lydia. And as he watched her kindness, her compassion, her cheerful smile even though she was exhausted, he fell in love with her all over again.

She lifted her hands to her face and rubbed it, turned as someone came alongside her. 'Your shift is nearly up. Just this last one and then I'll take over.'

His cue to place the basket he was carrying on the shelf, take out the single item it contained and place it on the conveyer.

He saw her gather herself for one last effort. Put the smile back in place, turn to wait for the goods to reach her. Saw the smile falter, the frown pucker her brow as she watched the tiny dark blue velvet-covered box move slowly towards her. The diamond solitaire at its heart sparking a rainbow of light.

Confused, she looked up. Saw him standing at the far end of the conveyer as, behind him, half a dozen shoppers stared open-mouthed. Rose slowly to her feet.

'Kal...'

'The ring was in my pocket when I returned to Umm al Sama, Lydia. I was sure that you knew, understood that the only woman I would take there would be my bride. But I wanted to give you a tangible token of my love. Something more than a dream.'

'I am not what you wanted.'

'Until I met you I didn't know what I wanted, but love is the star to every wandering bark, Lydia. You taught me that. I had been wandering all my life, without a star to guide me...' He sank to his knees. '*Ahebbak*, Lydia. I love you. I am begging you to marry me, to be my princess, my wife, my lover, the mother of my children, my soul, my life.'

The growing crowd of onlookers broke out into a spontaneous round of applause but it was Lydia who mattered.

'How is he?' she asked. 'Your grandfather?'

'Happy to be home. Thanks to you.'

'Then you have everything.'

'Everything but you.' He stood up, took the ring from the box, held it up, then touched it to each finger of her left hand, counting slowly in Arabic... '*Wahid, ithnan, thelatha, arba'a, khamsa...*'

'*Ithnan, ya habibi*—my beloved,' she said. '*Ahebbak*, Kalil. I love you.'

He slipped the ring onto the ring finger of her left hand, then walked around the checkout, took her in his arms and kissed her.

By this time they had brought the entire row of checkouts to a standstill. And the entire store was clapping.

'Maybe we had better leave, my love,' he said. 'These good people need to finish their shopping. And we have a wedding to arrange.'

*Daily Chronicle, 2nd March 2010*

## LADY ROSE LOOKALIKE MARRIES HER LORD

Lydia Young, who for ten years made regular appearances as a Lady Rose lookalike, was married today at Umm al Sama in Ramal Hamrah to Sheikh Kalil bin Zaki al-Khatib, nephew of the Emir.

Sheikh Kalil, who founded the international air freight company Kalzak Air Services, met Miss Young before Christmas and proposed after a whirlwind romance.

The bride's mother Mrs Glenys Young, who was formerly a seamstress for a London couturier, made her daughter's wedding dress from a bolt of cream silk that was a gift from the groom.

Four of the groom's sisters were attendants and his brother was best man. Family members and guests flew in from all over the world to be present at the ceremony, amongst them Lady Rose Napier and her fiancé billionaire businessman George Saxon. The groom's grandfather, who is gravely ill, rallied sufficiently to make a short speech at the reception.

The couple will spend their time between homes in London, Paris, New York and Ramal Hamrah.

*Bestselling author Lynne Graham is back with a fabulous new trilogy!*

## PREGNANT BRIDES

*Three ordinary girls—naive, but also honest and plucky...*

*Three fabulously wealthy, impossibly handsome and very ruthless men...*

*When opposites attract and passion leads to pregnancy... it can only mean marriage!*

*Available next month from Harlequin Presents®: the first installment*

# DESERT PRINCE, BRIDE OF INNOCENCE

\* \* \*

'THIS EVENING I'm flying to New York for two weeks,' Jasim imparted with a casualness that made her heart sink like a stone. 'That's why I had you brought here. I own this apartment and you'll be comfortable here while I'm abroad.'

'I can afford my own accommodation although I may not need it for long. I'll have another job by the time you get back—'

Jasim released a slightly harsh laugh. 'There's no need for you to look for another position. How would I ever see you? Don't you understand what I'm offering you?'

Elinor stood very still. 'No, I must be incredibly thick because I haven't quite worked out yet what you're offering me....'

His charismatic smile slashed his lean dark visage. 'Naturally, I want to take care of you....'

HPEX0110A

'No, thanks.' Elinor forced a smile and mentally willed him not to demean her with some sordid proposition. 'The only man who will ever take *care* of me with my agreement will be my husband. I'm willing to wait for you to come back but I'm not willing to be kept by you. I'm a very independent woman and what I give, I give freely.'

Jasim frowned. 'You make it all sound so serious.'

'What happened between us last night left pure chaos in its wake. Right now, I don't know whether I'm on my head or my heels. I'll stay for a while because I have nowhere else to go in the short term. So maybe it's good that you'll be away for a while.'

Jasim pulled out his wallet to extract a card. 'My private number,' he told her, presenting her with it as though it was a precious gift, which indeed it was. Many women would have done just about anything to gain access to that direct hotline to him, but his staff guarded his privacy with scrupulous care.

Before he could close the wallet, his blood ran cold in his veins. How could he have made such a serious oversight? What if he had got her pregnant? He knew that an unplanned pregnancy would engulf his life like an avalanche, crush his freedom and suffocate him. He barely stilled a shudder at the threat of such an outcome and thought how ironic it was that what his older brother had longed and prayed for to secure the line to the throne should strike Jasim as an absolute disaster....

\* \* \*

*What will proud Prince Jasim do if Elinor is expecting his royal baby? Perhaps an arranged marriage is the only solution! But will Elinor agree? Find out in DESERT PRINCE, BRIDE OF INNOCENCE by Lynne Graham [#2884], available from Harlequin Presents® in January 2010.*

HPEX0110B

HARLEQUIN® *Romance*®

 ESCAPE AROUND *the* WORLD

*Dream destinations, whirlwind weddings!*

# *The Daredevil Tycoon*
## *by*
# BARBARA McMAHON

A hot-air balloon race with Amalia Catalon's
sexy daredevil boss, Rafael Sandoval, is only the
beginning of her exciting Spanish adventure....

*Available in January 2010
wherever books are sold.*

HR17632

# REQUEST YOUR FREE BOOKS!
## 2 FREE NOVELS PLUS 2
# FREE GIFTS!

HARLEQUIN® *Romance*®

## From the Heart, For the Heart

**YES!** Please send me 2 FREE Harlequin® Romance novels and my 2 FREE gifts (gifts are worth about $10). After receiving them, if I don't wish to receive any more books, I can return the shipping statement marked "cancel". If I don't cancel, I will receive 4 brand-new novels every month and be billed just $3.84 per book in the U.S. or $4.24 per book in Canada. That's a savings of at least 15% off the cover price! It's quite a bargain! Shipping and handling is just 50¢ per book.* I understand that accepting the 2 free books and gifts places me under no obligation to buy anything. I can always return a shipment and cancel at any time. Even if I never buy another book, the two free books and gifts are mine to keep forever.

114 HDN EYU3  314 HDN EYKG

| Name | (PLEASE PRINT) | |
| --- | --- | --- |
| Address | | Apt. # |
| City | State/Prov. | Zip/Postal Code |

Signature (if under 18, a parent or guardian must sign)

### Mail to the **Harlequin** Reader Service:
**IN U.S.A.:** P.O. Box 1867, Buffalo, NY 14240-1867
**IN CANADA:** P.O. Box 609, Fort Erie, Ontario  L2A 5X3

Not valid to current subscribers of Harlequin Romance books.

**Are you a subscriber of Harlequin Romance books
and want to receive the larger-print edition?
Call 1-800-873-8635 today!**

HR09R

## HARLEQUIN® HISTORICAL:
### Where love is timeless

**From chivalrous knights to roguish rakes, look for the variety Harlequin® Historical has to offer every month.**

HARLEQUIN *Romance*

## Coming Next Month

### Available January 12, 2010

**Fall in love in 2010—with Harlequin® Romance!**

#### #4141 THE ITALIAN'S FORGOTTEN BABY Raye Morgan
*Baby on Board*
Marco has lost two weeks of his life and wants them back. After an accident on holiday left him with amnesia, he's returned to the beautiful island to find his memories—and a baby bombshell!

#### #4142 THE DAREDEVIL TYCOON Barbara McMahon
*Escape Around the World*
A hot-air balloon race with her daredevil boss, Rafael, is only the beginning of Amalia's Spanish adventure....

#### #4143 JUST MARRIED! Cara Colter and Shirley Jump
You're invited to two very special weddings! Grab a glass of champagne for bridesmaid Samantha's big day and a handful of confetti for when best man Colton ties the knot!

#### #4144 THE GIRL FROM HONEYSUCKLE FARM Jessica Steele
*In Her Shoes...*
Phinn isn't fooled by eligible bachelor Ty's good looks, and sparks fly when she discovers he's the hotshot London financier who bought her beloved Honeysuckle Farm.

#### #4145 ONE DANCE WITH THE COWBOY Donna Alward
Cowboy Drew left Larch Valley promising Jen he'd return. When he didn't, she moved on.... Now Drew's back! Could *Cowboys and Confetti* be on the horizon? Find out in the first of a brand-new duet.

#### #4146 HIRED: SASSY ASSISTANT Nina Harrington
*9 to 5*
Medic Kyle has swapped the wilds of Nepal for Lulu's English country house. He wants to publish her famous mother's diaries—that is if he can get this sassy assistant to play ball.